BOB DYLAN
THE LYRICS 1961–2012
鲍勃·迪伦诗歌集

红色天空下

[美] 鲍勃·迪伦　著

西川　李皖　厄土　陈震　译

广西师范大学出版社
·桂林·

HONGSE TIANKONG XIA

LYRICS: 1961-2012

Copyright © 2016, Bob Dylan

All rights reserved.

著作权合同登记号桂图登字：20-2017-053 号

图书在版编目（CIP）数据

鲍勃·迪伦诗歌集：1961—2012. 红色天空下：汉
英对照 /（美）鲍勃·迪伦著；西川等译. —桂林：
广西师范大学出版社，2017.6（2018.7 重印）

书名原文：LYRICS: 1961-2012

ISBN 978-7-5495-9688-1

Ⅰ．①鲍… Ⅱ．①鲍…②西… Ⅲ．①诗集－美国－
现代－汉、英 Ⅳ．①I712.25

中国版本图书馆 CIP 数据核字（2017）第 078987 号

出　版：广西师范大学出版社
　　　　　广西桂林市五里店路 9 号　邮政编码：541004
网　址：http://www.bbtpress.com
出版人：张艺兵
发　行：广西师范大学出版社
　　　　　电话：（0773）2802178
印　刷：山东临沂新华印刷物流集团有限责任公司印刷
　　　　　山东临沂高新技术产业开发区新华路
　　　　　邮政编码：276017
开　本：740 mm × 1 092 mm　1/32
印　张：7.25　　　　字数：80 千字
版　次：2017 年 6 月第 1 版　　2018 年 7 月第 3 次
定　价：25.00 元

目 录

烂醉如泥

妙境深处

哦，仁慈

红色天空下

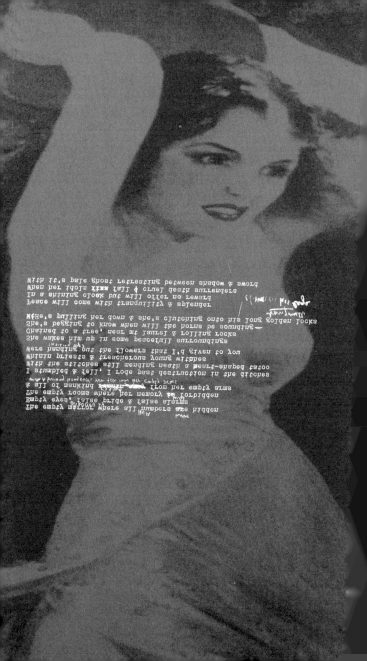

烂醉如泥
Knocked Out Loaded

西川　译

　　20 世纪 80 年代中期的鲍勃·迪伦似乎陷入灵感匮乏的困境中，一连串发行的专辑都风评不佳，1986 年 7 月 14 日发行的第二十四张录音室专辑《烂醉如泥》也未能例外。这张专辑中除去三首翻唱，余下的五首，三首系与其他创作者合作，仅两首由迪伦独自作曲，原创色彩并不浓厚。整张专辑的方向与特色不甚鲜明，令人很难把握到其脉络。正如专辑名字《烂醉如泥》，迪伦将各个时期的作品胡乱拼凑在一起，成了融合他历来多种风格和特点的大杂烩：《自由不羁的鲍勃·迪伦》中旁征博引的诗意，《重访 61 号公路》中的超现实景象和蓝调摇滚风格，《轨道上的血》中的抒情主题以及"基督教三部曲"中的宗教色彩……

　　幸运的是，这张专辑有一首经典之作能够挽回颜面，也就是长达十一分钟的《布朗斯维尔姑娘》。旋律部分取用《帝国滑稽剧》未收录的作品——《新丹维尔姑娘》（*New Danville*

Girl）叠录而成，显然新旧两"姑娘"都带有迪伦的偶像伍迪·格思里（Woody Guthrie）《丹维尔姑娘》（*Danville Girl*）的影子。歌词方面，迪伦又与美国剧作家萨姆·谢泼德（Sam Shepard）联手，重新填写，讲述一个好莱坞西部爱情片式的美丽故事，成为如今所见的《布朗斯维尔姑娘》，一首能与《荒芜巷》和《黑钻石湾》相提并论的长篇叙事歌谣。

编者

漂离岸边已太远

我原本不知道你会离开
或你以为你曾同谁在讲话
我以为或许我们是互不拖欠的
又或许你对我有亏欠 [1]

我所有的钱都寄给了你
就像我做过的在从前
我努力够到你，心肝
但你漂离岸边已太远

漂离岸边已太远
漂离岸边已太远
漂离岸边已太远
漂离岸边已太远

我将不会在这湍流中迷失
我不喜欢猫捉老鼠的游戏

---

1. 以上两行歌词源自美国西部电影《怒河》（ *In Bend of the River*，1952）的台词。

绅士不会上一个女仆
尤其是在他父亲的家里 [1]

我从来猜不出你的分量，宝
你是我马子我从不这么喊
我老想你是直来直去的，宝
但你漂离岸边已太远

漂离岸边已太远
漂离岸边已太远
漂离岸边已太远
漂离岸边已太远

嗯这些日子这些地道在闹鬼
水桶底部也传出怪声音
为一个心愿有时我长年等待
没人会像你一般幸运

我不再胡思乱想为什么
你不再同我一起玩儿
任何时候你都会沉没

---

1. 以上两行歌词源自美国爱情电影《龙凤配》（*Sabrina*，1954）的台词。

因你漂离岸边已太远

漂离岸边已太远
漂离岸边已太远
漂离岸边已太远
漂离岸边已太远

你我曾是完整的一对儿
能给你的我已全部给出
我们不是犯了错误，甜人儿
我们自己就是错误

我已扯断电话线，心肝
你不能在战争中去遛弯儿
我可以一人走到头，心肝
你漂离岸边已太远

Driftin' Too Far from Shore

I didn't know that you'd be leavin'
Or who you thought you were talkin' to
I figure maybe we're even
Or maybe I'm one up on you

I send you all my money
Just like I did before
I tried to reach you honey
But you're driftin' too far from shore

Driftin' too far from shore
Driftin' too far from shore
Driftin' too far from shore
Driftin' too far from shore

I ain't gonna get lost in this current
I don't like playing cat and mouse
No gentleman likes making love to a servant
Especially when he's in his father's house

I never could guess your weight, baby
Never needed to call you my whore
I always thought you were straight, baby
But you're driftin' too far from shore

Driftin' too far from shore
Driftin' too far from shore
Driftin' too far from shore
Driftin' too far from shore

Well these times and these tunnels are haunted
The bottom of the barrel is too
I waited years sometimes for what I wanted
Everybody can't be as lucky as you

Never no more do I wonder
Why you don't never play with me anymore
At any moment you could go under
'Cause you're driftin' too far from shore

Driftin' too far from shore
Driftin' too far from shore
Driftin' too far from shore
Driftin' too far from shore

You and me we had completeness
I give you all of what I could provide
We weren't on the wrong side, sweetness
We were the wrong side

I've already ripped out the phones, honey
You can't walk the streets in a war
I can finish this alone honey
You're driftin' too far from shore

也许某一天

也许某一天你将舒心

当你丢失了一切你将无物可藏

当你浏览万物仿佛穿过铁道

也许你会求我把你带回

也许某一天你会发现每个人在别人看来都是傻瓜

也许到那时你就明白我为了冷静下来付出了啥

也许某一天你孤身一人时

你将知道我对你的爱从来不属于我自己

也许某一天你将无处可去

你将回望并好奇你烧毁的桥梁

你将回望片刻在灯火变暗之际

你将看出你跟我在一起时比跟他更惬意

穿过敌意的城市和不友好的镇子

身上三十块[1]，就是没钱

也许有一天，你会晓得

不劳而获是人人的算盘儿

---

1. 指涉《圣经》中犹大出卖耶稣，得血钱银币三十块。

也许某一天你将记起你的感受

在棉花带 [1] 当月亮上有血光

当我们俩，宝，要通过某个考验

我们可以做得最好但我们谁都不会做

我本该知道，宝，我本该让你把话说清

我猜我也是昏了头，不够多愁善感

也许某一天，你会相信当我说

我想要你，宝，一切的一切

也许某一天你将听到一个声音来自高处

问："你为谁而生，你为谁而死？" [2]

原谅我，宝，为我未做之事

为我不曾冲破卧室之门来爱你 [3]

为我曾总是迷恋右钩拳

为我从不想回家直到兜里没有一分钱

也许某一天你回首会看出

我让你跟随我变得如此轻松

---

1. 棉花带，美国东南部产棉地带。

2.《新约·哥林多后书》5:15："并且他替众人死，是叫那些活着的人不再为自己而活，乃为替他们死而复活的主而活。"注释凡涉《圣经》处，译文一律引自和合本，供大致的参照；《圣经》中屡见者，一般仅引一条。

3. 源自美国剧情电影《鸳鸯谱》(*Separate Tables*，1958）的台词。

也许某一天我将无话可说

我像你一样快乐，宝，我只是笨嘴拙舌

永远别酣睡别等着闪电劈来

你没理由说咱俩不是老想到一块儿

你说你要去旧金山待上几个月

我一直喜欢那里，我曾去那里参加聚会[1]

也许某一天你会千真万确地看到

与我对你的爱相比没有更伟大的爱

---

1. 源自美国黑色电影《漩涡之外》（*Out of the Past*，1947）的台词。

Maybe Someday

Maybe someday you'll be satisfied
When you've lost everything you'll have nothing left to hide
When you're through running over things like you're
   walking 'cross the tracks
Maybe you'll beg me to take you back
Maybe someday you'll find out everybody's somebody's fool
Maybe then you'll realize what it would have taken to keep
   me cool
Maybe someday when you're by yourself alone
You'll know the love that I had for you was never my own

Maybe someday you'll have nowhere to turn
You'll look back and wonder 'bout the bridges you have
   burned
You'll look back sometime when the lights grow dim
And you'll see you look much better with me than you do
   with him
Through hostile cities and unfriendly towns
Thirty pieces of silver, no money down
Maybe someday, you will understand
That something for nothing is everybody's plan

Maybe someday you'll remember what you felt
When there was blood on the moon in the cotton belt
When both of us, baby, were going through some sort of
   a test
Neither one of us could do what we do best
I should have known better, baby, I should have called your
   bluff

I guess I was too off the handle, not sentimental enough
Maybe someday, you'll believe me when I say
That I wanted you, baby, in every kind of way

Maybe someday you'll hear a voice from on high
Sayin', "For whose sake did you live, for whose sake did you
    die?"
Forgive me, baby, for what I didn't do
For not breakin' down no bedroom door to get at you
Always was a sucker for the right cross
Never wanted to go home 'til the last cent was lost
Maybe someday you will look back and see
That I made it so easy for you to follow me

Maybe someday there'll be nothing to tell
I'm just as happy as you, baby, I just can't say it so well
Never slumbered or slept or waited for lightning to strike
There's no excuse for you to say that we don't think alike
You said you were goin' to Frisco, stay a couple of months
I always like San Francisco, I was there for a party once
Maybe someday you'll see that it's true
There was no greater love than what I had for you

布朗斯维尔[1] 姑娘

（与萨姆·谢泼德合作）

有这么个电影[2] 我曾经看过
讲一个男人骑马过沙漠，主演是格里高利·派克
一个饥饿的男孩为了出名把他一枪撂倒
镇上的人们想要吊死那男孩并把他撕烂

嗯，警察局长把那孩子打得血里呼啦
这枪手将死，喘着最后一口气，瘫在阳光下
"给他松绑放他走，让他去说他堂堂正正拔枪比我快
我要叫他尝尝这滋味：面对死亡，每时每刻"

嗯，这事儿我一直在面对，它朝我滚来涌来
你看它像铁球铁链一样劈头盖脸
你看我不能相信我们已活了如此之久却依然相距如此遥远
对你的记忆像一列火车滚滚而来追踪着我

---

1. 布朗斯维尔，美国得克萨斯州南部城市，位于美墨边境。
2. 指美国西部电影《枪手》（ The Gunfighter，1950 ），格里高利·派克在片中饰演一个为声名所累的枪手。

还记得那天在多彩沙漠[1]你来会我
开着你的破福特，穿着你的厚底儿高跟鞋
我永远弄不懂你为啥偏选那个地方来见面
啊，但你是对的。太棒了当我坐到方向盘前

嗯，我们整夜开车去了圣安东[2]
我们睡在阿拉莫[3]附近，你的皮肤好细柔
一路开到墨西哥你去找医生再没回来
我本该去找你但我不想让我的脑袋被打开花

嗯，我们开着这辆车，太阳升上落基山脉
我现在知道她不是你但她在这，她灵魂中有黑暗的节奏
但我也是身在悬崖边上，再无心思回忆我是你唯一男人
　的时候
她也不想提醒我。她知道这辆车终将报废

布朗斯维尔姑娘布朗斯维尔卷发
皓齿如珍珠闪烁如高悬的明月一轮
布朗斯维尔姑娘，带我走过全世界

---

1. 多彩沙漠，位于美国亚利桑那州东北部。
2. 圣安东，即美国得克萨斯州城市圣安东尼奥。
3. 阿拉莫，圣安东尼奥一座由传教站扩建而成的要塞。

布朗斯维尔姑娘，你是我甜蜜的爱人

嗯，我们穿过锅把区[1]，然后一头扎向阿马里洛[2]
我们停在亨利·波特住过的地方。城外一英里他有间破屋
露比在后院晾衣裳，红头发束在脑后。她见我们一路烟
　　尘开过来
她说："亨利不在但你们进来吧，他过一小会就回来"

然后她说到岁月的艰辛，说到她想搭车回到她出来的地方
但你知道，每次一涉及钱她就换过话题
她说："欢迎来到活死人的地方。"你会感到她已心碎
她说："即使这里的旧货交易会也变得越来越烂"

"你们一路走要走多远？"露比对我们叹道
"我们一直走直到车轮子跑掉并燃烧
直到车漆被太阳剥落，车座套磨烂，直到水蝮蛇死掉"
露比笑言："啊，看呐，有些孩子就是不长进"

这是那电影中的一些事，嗯我就是没办法摆脱
但我忘了为啥我会在电影里，或我演的该是哪一个

---

1. 锅把区，美国得克萨斯州北部的柄状狭长区域。
2. 阿马里洛，美国得克萨斯州北部城市。

只记得这是格里高利·派克的片子，和人们的举手投足
他们中很多人好像都是我这副样子

布朗斯维尔姑娘布朗斯维尔卷发
皓齿如珍珠闪烁如高悬的明月一轮
布朗斯维尔姑娘，带我走过全世界
布朗斯维尔姑娘，你是我甜蜜的爱人

嗯，他们在找那个梳着蓬帕杜发型[1]的人
我穿过大街时枪声大作
我不知我是该藏还是该跑，所以我拔腿就跑
"我们在教堂院子里堵住了他。"我听见有人在喊叫

嗯，你看到我的照片刊载于《科珀斯克里斯蒂[2]论坛报》，
　下注"无不在场证明者"
你冒险为我作证，说我和你在一起
我看到你在法官面前崩溃，流下真正的眼泪
这是我见过的最好的表演

---

1. 蓬帕杜发型，即"猫王"埃尔维斯·普雷斯利经典发型，将刘海向后高高梳起。
2. 科珀斯克里斯蒂，美国得克萨斯州南部港口城市，本意为"圣体"或"圣体节"。

看呐我这人从不爱冒犯别人，但有时你会发现你已越界

噢如果那儿有个想法挺独特，我就会立即使用它

你看，我觉得挺好，但我不想说太多。如果你就在

　　我身旁告诉我该如何做

我会整个感觉好得多

嗯，我在雨中排队看格里高利·派克的电影

是呀，但你知道这不是我想看的那一部

他又拍了新片，我都不知它讲的啥

但我就是想看他，所以会排队，啥电影都行

布朗斯维尔姑娘布朗斯维尔卷发

皓齿如珍珠闪烁如高悬的明月一轮

布朗斯维尔姑娘，带我走过全世界

布朗斯维尔姑娘，你是我甜蜜的爱人

你看，事情的结果从不如你所愿，有趣

这个亨利·波特，我们唯一确知的是这并非他的姓名

你看宝，我喜欢你身上的某些东西，对这个世界来说

　　总是太精彩

就像你总说喜欢我身上的某些东西，被我抛在法国区 [1]

---

1. 法国区，位于美国路易斯安那州新奥尔良。

奇怪苦在一块儿的人们的关系何以比那些满足者之间的
　　关系更密切
我没啥可后悔，我走后他们可对我大谈而特谈
你总说人们的所为并非其所信，他们只做最方便的事，
　　然后懊悔
而我总说："跟我混，宝，但愿屋顶安然无恙"

我看过一部电影，我想是看过两遍
我忘了我曾经是谁或我曾在哪里
只记得它由格里高利·派克主演，他枪不离身，却被人
　　从背后一枪打来
那好像是很久以前，在星星被毁掉之前很久

布朗斯维尔姑娘布朗斯维尔卷发
皓齿如珍珠闪烁如高悬的明月一轮
布朗斯维尔姑娘，带我走过全世界
布朗斯维尔姑娘，你是我甜蜜的爱人

Brownsville Girl
(with Sam Shepard)

Well, there was this movie I seen one time
About a man riding 'cross the desert and it starred Gregory
Peck
He was shot down by a hungry kid trying to make a name
for himself
The townspeople wanted to crush that kid down and string
him up by the neck

Well, the marshal, now he beat that kid to a bloody pulp
As the dying gunfighter lay in the sun and gasped for his last
breath
"Turn him loose, let him go, let him say he outdrew me fair
and square
I want him to feel what it's like to every moment face his
death"

Well, I keep seeing this stuff and it just comes a-rolling in
And you know it blows right through me like a ball and
chain
You know I can't believe we've lived so long and are still so
far apart
The memory of you keeps callin' after me like a rollin' train

I can still see the day that you came to me on the painted desert
In your busted down Ford and your platform heels
I could never figure out why you chose that particular place
to meet

Ah, but you were right. It was perfect as I got in behind the wheel

Well, we drove that car all night into San Anton'
And we slept near the Alamo, your skin was so tender and soft
Way down in Mexico you went out to find a doctor and you never came back
I would have gone on after you but I didn't feel like letting my head get blown off

Well, we're drivin' this car and the sun is comin' up over the Rockies
Now I know she ain't you but she's here and she's got that dark rhythm in her soul
But I'm too over the edge and I ain't in the mood anymore to remember the times when I was your only man
And she don't want to remind me. She knows this car would go out of control

Brownsville girl with your Brownsville curls
Teeth like pearls shining like the moon above
Brownsville girl, show me all around the world
Brownsville girl, you're my honey love

Well, we crossed the panhandle and then we headed towards Amarillo
We pulled up where Henry Porter used to live. He owned a wreckin' lot outside of town about a mile
Ruby was in the backyard hanging clothes, she had her red hair tied back. She saw us come rolling up in a trail of dust
She said, "Henry ain't here but you can come on in, he'll be back in a little while"

Then she told us how times were tough and about how she
    was thinkin' of bummin' a ride back to from where she started
But ya know, she changed the subject every time money
    came up
She said, "Welcome to the land of the living dead."
    You could tell she was so broken hearted
She said, "Even the swap meets around here are getting
    pretty corrupt"

"How far are y'all going?" Ruby asked us with a sigh
"We're going all the way 'til the wheels fall off and burn
'Til the sun peels the paint and the seat covers fade and the
    water moccasin dies"
Ruby just smiled and said, "Ah, you know some babies
    never learn"

Something about that movie though, well I just can't get it
    out of my head
But I can't remember why I was in it or what part I was
    supposed to play
All I remember about it was Gregory Peck and the way
    people moved
And a lot of them seemed to be lookin' my way

Brownsville girl with your Brownsville curls
Teeth like pearls shining like the moon above
Brownsville girl, show me all around the world
Brownsville girl, you're my honey love

Well, they were looking for somebody with a pompadour
I was crossin' the street when shots rang out
I didn't know whether to duck or to run, so I ran

"We got him cornered in the churchyard," I heard somebody
    shout

Well, you saw my picture in the *Corpus Christi Tribune*.
    Underneath it, it said, "A man with no alibi"
You went out on a limb to testify for me, you said I was
    with you
Then when I saw you break down in front of the judge and
    cry real tears
It was the best acting I saw anybody do

Now I've always been the kind of person that doesn't like to
    trespass but sometimes you just find yourself over the line
Oh if there's an original thought out there, I could use it
    right now
You know, I feel pretty good, but that ain't sayin' much.
    I could feel a whole lot better
If you were just here by my side to show me how

Well, I'm standin' in line in the rain to see a movie starring
    Gregory Peck
Yeah, but you know it's not the one that I had in mind
He's got a new one out now, I don't even know what it's about
But I'll see him in anything so I'll stand in line

Brownsville girl with your Brownsville curls
Teeth like pearls shining like the moon above
Brownsville girl, show me all around the world
Brownsville girl, you're my honey love

You know, it's funny how things never turn out the way
    you had 'em planned

The only thing we knew for sure about Henry Porter
is that his name wasn't Henry Porter
And you know there was somethin' about you baby that I
liked that was always too good for this world
Just like you always said there was somethin' about me you
liked that I left behind in the French Quarter

Strange how people who suffer together have stronger
connections than people who are most content
I don't have any regrets, they can talk about me plenty when
I'm gone
You always said people don't do what they believe in,
they just do what's most convenient, then they repent
And I always said, "Hang on to me, baby, and let's hope
that the roof stays on"

There was a movie I seen one time, I think I sat through it
twice
I don't remember who I was or where I was bound
All I remember about it was it starred Gregory Peck, he
wore a gun and he was shot in the back
Seems like a long time ago, long before the stars were torn
down

Brownsville girl with your Brownsville curls
Teeth like pearls shining like the moon above
Brownsville girl, show me all around the world
Brownsville girl, you're my honey love

我为你着迷

（与卡罗尔·拜尔·塞杰尔[1]合作）

有些关于你的事我无法忘怀

不知我为此还能有多少承载

宝，我为你着迷

在赤裸的夜晚我喝到昏脑昏头

你的光我注意到了在我最后的梦碎之后

宝，哦，多棒的故事我能讲

见到你真好，你读我如读书

若你想找到我，你知道我在哪里住

宝，我还住在那家旅馆

我想帮你但我自己有点麻烦

我明天会电你若我离电话不太远

宝，我困在了天堂和地狱之间

---

1. 卡罗尔·拜尔·塞杰尔（Carol Bayer Sager, 1947— ），美国作词人、歌手和画家。据塞杰尔说，她为这首歌创作的歌词大部分未被采用，但迪伦表示这首歌少了她就写不出来。

但我会回来，我命不该绝
你将永难摆脱我只要你活着
宝，你难道还看不出么

现在凌晨四点，小鸟在叽叽喳喳
我盯着你的照片，听见你说话
宝，你的话像铃儿在我脑子里振响

你去的每个地方都足以让人心碎
有的人总是受伤，有地方总是着火
你太飒了难以把控，你一句誓言都没守过
我信任你，宝，你现在也可以信任我

擦干你的泪眼，宝，转过身来
别以为没有吻别我就会离开
宝，还有什么话要说却没说？

我会再见你当我不再那么魂不守舍
也许下一次我会让死人埋死人 [1]
宝，我还能说些什么？

1.《新约·马太福音》8:22："耶稣说：'任凭死人埋葬他们的死人，你跟从我吧！'"

嗯沙漠很热，山被诅咒

但愿我不会渴死在

宝，离水井两英尺远的地方

Under Your Spell
(with Carol Bayer Sager)

Somethin' about you that I can't shake
Don't know how much more of this I can take
Baby, I'm under your spell

I was knocked out and loaded in the naked night
When my last dream exploded, I noticed your light
Baby, oh what a story I could tell

It's been nice seeing you, you read me like a book
If you ever want to reach me, you know where to look
Baby, I'll be at the same hotel

I'd like to help you but I'm in a bit of a jam
I'll call you tomorrow if there's phones where I am
Baby, caught between heaven and hell

But I will be back, I will survive
You'll never get rid of me as long as you're alive
Baby, can't you tell

Well it's four in the morning by the sound of the birds
I'm starin' at your picture, I'm hearin' your words
Baby, they ring in my head like a bell

Everywhere you go it's enough to break hearts
Someone always gets hurt, a fire always starts
You were too hot to handle, you were breaking every vow
I trusted you baby, you can trust me now

Turn back baby, wipe your eye
Don't think I'm leaving here without a kiss goodbye
Baby, is there anything left to tell?

I'll see you later when I'm not so out of my head
Maybe next time I'll let the dead bury the dead
Baby, what more can I tell?

Well the desert is hot, the mountain is cursed
Pray that I don't die of thirst
Baby, two feet from the well

五指成掌，五人为帮
（时辰到，兄弟！）[1]

五指成掌，五人为帮

五指成掌，五人为帮

五指成掌，五人为帮

五指成掌，五人为帮

在这些蠢材控制的街区

毫无自由或自尊可言

要么挨一刀要么坐一趟牢

也没啥别的可期盼

他们杀死这里捍卫自己权利的人

体制真是太他妈的腐败

总都一个样子，问题的实质

是谁的关系更厉害

五指成掌，五人为帮

------

1. 这首歌是迪伦为美国同名电影《四海小兄弟》(*Band of the Hand*，1986) 而作的，所述内容与影片情节有关。

五指成掌，五人为帮

五指成掌，五人为帮

五指成掌，五人为帮

黑人白人都

把其他孩子的命偷走

财富是污秽的衣服[1]

如此色情，如此无爱国情

如此对星条旗全神倾注

善妖惑的人渣支使着哑巴

把小孩儿都坑成骗徒、奴隶

拜嗑得死嗨的毒贩子做大佬、大师

这帮东西都该送进坟里

五指成掌，五人为帮

五指成掌，五人为帮

五指成掌，五人为帮

五指成掌，五人为帮

听我说大毒枭先生

1.《旧约·以赛亚书》64:6："所有的义都像污秽的衣服……"

这许是你在床上最后一晚的安稳
那些皮条客谋财路，破政客受贿赂
你却收买不了我们

我们要炸掉你巫毒教的巢穴
不带一丝遗憾看着它燃烧
我们得了势，我们是新政府
你只是还不曾知道

五指成掌，五人为帮
五指成掌，五人为帮
五指成掌，五人为帮
五指成掌，五人为帮

为了我所有从越南回来的兄弟
从第二次世界大战走来的伯父
我得说现在是时候倒数了
我们要尽本应法律来尽的义务

而为了你可人儿
我知道你的经历苦不堪言
但总有一天你会在梦中提起

当你这样时，我想在你身边 [1]

五指成掌，五人为帮

五指成掌，五人为帮

五指成掌，五人为帮

五指成掌，五人为帮

---

1. 以上两行歌词源自美国黑色电影《醒时尖叫》(*I Wake Up Screaming*，1941）的台词。

Band of the Hand
(It's Hell Time, Man!)

Band of the hand
Band of the hand
Band of the hand
Band of the hand

Down these streets the fools rule
There's no freedom or self respect
A knife's point or a trip to the joint
Is about all you can expect

They kill people here who stand up for their rights
The system's just too damned corrupt
It's always the same, the name of the game
Is who do you know higher up

Band of the hand
Band of the hand
Band of the hand
Band of the hand

The blacks and the whites
Steal the other kids' lives
Wealth is a filthy rag
So erotic so unpatriotic
So wrapped up in the American flag

The witchcraft scum exploiting the dumb

Turns children into crooks and slaves
Whose heroes and healers are real stoned dealers
Who should be put in their graves

Band of the hand
Band of the hand
Band of the hand
Band of the hand

Listen to me Mr. Pusherman
This might be your last night in a bed so soft
There are pimps on the make, politicians on the take
You can't pay us off

We're gonna blow up your home of Voodoo
And watch it burn without any regret
We got the power, we're the new government
You just don't know it yet

Band of the hand
Band of the hand
Band of the hand
Band of the hand

For all of my brothers from Vietnam
And my uncles from World War II
I've got to say that it's countdown time now
We're gonna do what the law should do

And for you pretty baby
I know your story is too painful to share
One day though you'll be talking in your sleep
And when you do, I wanna be there

Band of the hand
Band of the hand
Band of the hand
Band of the hand

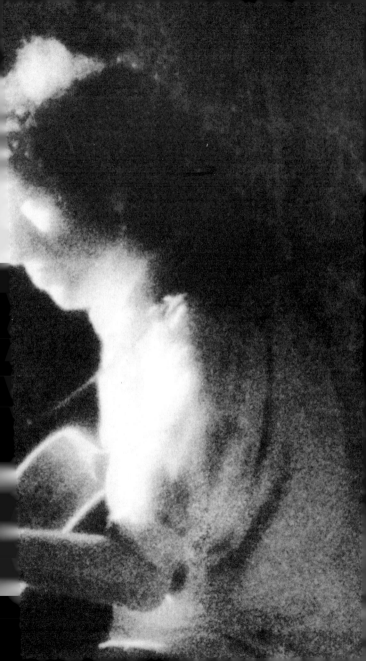

for him and it turned one sweet day into a raging storm
the ~~bread~~ **priest** was blacker on the 7th day til the ~~Rey~~
and waltzed from a sloping floor **waltz**
what ~~I~~ began, you couldn't ~~finish~~
~~she tilted~~ that to me **false**
you could [You thought she was a party doll]
(You fell for) Her personality and I was I was
A hound dog tossed beyond the ~~tup again~~ just along for the
As I was ~~As I'd just met~~ ~~and I parked my Unicorn~~
That's not the way it happened, ~~Mister~~ ~~we at the~~
I thought you been someone else **Prel X**
It must've BEEN the mask you wore **done**

for I figured (I supposed) I've lost you anyway
& why — from the give
there would be just yo voices & online free
(try my to tradezation wave
you must think I'm someone else / I ~~win~~ saw you
I didn't called you for days why, it went ~~became~~ ~~used to~~
I knew what we were going to say ~~you went had to each~~
(creeps across the rooftops, but I hadn't memorized my (Goodbye)
I figured I lost you anyway **part of the speech**
So I pulled up stakes and went ~~for~~ **broke**
It didn't strike me very funny **focus** I focused
We didn't speak for days ~~and~~ , it must've been the cats had
they put ~~the~~ our ~~& perhaps~~ **got our tongue**
Fixed in my own dreams outcome
And I figured I lost you anyway ~~and when I lost you bac~~
And that you thought it all a joke it all came clear
But it didn't strike me very funny that to

I thought you were ~~pisst~~ but you thought it was scratches
For I figured I lost you anyway I was on
So what be the use I wonder & you were lose
In order to get ~~tm~~ to you, ~~I ame~~ I'd just have to
I'd have to use some ~~stale~~ excuse I come upon some
It don — funns (It just stuck me kinda funny
I didn't call you for days & days and it wasn't cause
(We hadn't talked for) Cat had my tongue
I didn't talk for days & day 2d it wasn't cause the cat
It was just that everyting I said was had got my tongue
We didn't talk for days and ~~never~~ ~~took~~ I say this words were
It Aint my fault nobody ever took the time to teach me gone
~~taught me how to forgive~~
Blet ~~cause~~ as take me for a fool

妙境深处
Down in the Groove

李皖　译（郝佳　校）

　　《妙境深处》是鲍勃·迪伦的第二十五张录音室专辑，发行于 1988 年 5 月。

　　此专辑收录了迪伦的十首作品，在曲目选择上几经反复，制作时间跨度长达六年。除两首迪伦原创、两首迪伦参与合作的作品外，其余六首均为翻唱之作。评论界普遍认为，这是迪伦水准以下的作品，《滚石》杂志更是将其列为迪伦最差的专辑。

　　此专辑的翻唱曲目甚多，难免会给人仓促拼凑之感。但有一种微弱的声音认为，这些作品虽非迪伦所创，却在一定程度上呈现了迪伦奇异、丰富的创作资源，并将他从可能正在固化的个人创作中拉出来，引向新的领域。虽然，这确实是不成熟的过渡，但对一位永不停息、一直在寻求自我超越的巨匠而言，这种向后的徘徊是必要的，其结果也是积极的。

　　本书收录了该专辑中两首迪伦的原创作品。其中《死亡不是终结》是迪伦 1983 年《异教徒》专辑中的弃用之作，当时迪伦深受基督教教义影响，因而此曲颇具宗教色彩。另一首《做了个关于你的梦，宝贝》则"回收"自 1987 年迪伦所出演的歌舞片《火之心》（Hearts of Fire）的插曲。相比起迪伦之前的情歌，此曲似乎更为浅显，像是美国普通的情歌。此外，本书还收录了《火之心》的另一首插曲《一夜又一夜》，其与《做了个关于你的梦，宝贝》同调，但歌词似是草草写就，收尾略显仓促。总的来说，这三首歌曲讲的是人人都能切的题、人人均可感的话，颇为通俗易懂，容易引起大众的共鸣。

李皖

死亡不是终结

当你又悲哀又孤独
一个朋友都没有
记住吧死亡不是终结
当你认为神圣的一切
倒塌下来，无可挽救
记住吧死亡不是终结
不是终结，不是终结
请记住死亡不是终结

当你站在十字路口
心中茫然无解
记住吧死亡不是终结
当你所有的梦已破灭
不知道弯道后会是什么
记住吧死亡不是终结
不是终结，不是终结
请记住死亡不是终结

当乌云集于你四周
暴雨倾盆而下

记住吧死亡不是终结

当没有人施以援手

给你安慰

记住吧死亡不是终结

不是终结，不是终结

请记住死亡不是终结

啊，生命之树常青

于灵魂永存之地

明亮的救赎之光照耀着

黑暗虚无的天空

当城市全烧起来

焚烧着人的肉身

记住吧死亡不是终结

当你到处搜寻

也难找到一个守法公民

记住吧死亡不是终结

不是终结，不是终结

请记住死亡不是终结

Death Is Not the End

When you're sad and when you're lonely
And you haven't got a friend
Just remember that death is not the end
And all that you've held sacred
Falls down and does not mend
Just remember that death is not the end
Not the end, not the end
Just remember that death is not the end

When you're standing at the crossroads
That you cannot comprehend
Just remember that death is not the end
And all your dreams have vanished
And you don't know what's up the bend
Just remember that death is not the end
Not the end, not the end
Just remember that death is not the end

When the storm clouds gather 'round you
And heavy rains descend
Just remember that death is not the end
And there's no one there to comfort you
With a helpin' hand to lend
Just remember that death is not the end
Not the end, not the end
Just remember that death is not the end

Oh, the tree of life is growing
Where the spirit never dies

And the bright light of salvation shines
In dark and empty skies

When the cities are on fire
With the burning flesh of men
Just remember that death is not the end
And you search in vain to find
Just one law-abiding citizen
Just remember that death is not the end
Not the end, not the end
Just remember that death is not the end

做了个关于你的梦，宝贝

我要见你宝贝，我不管
在什么地方，宝贝，这由你来定

我做了个关于你的梦，宝贝
做了个关于你的梦，宝贝
昨天深夜你旋转着，掠过我的心头

你的脚步节奏疯狂
你一开口我就紧张万分

我做了个关于你的梦，宝贝
做了个关于你的梦，宝贝
昨天深夜你旋转着，掠过我的心头

站在公路边，你打手势让我停下
说带我一程大叔，去最近的镇子

我做了个关于你的梦，宝贝
做了个关于你的梦，宝贝
昨天深夜你旋转着，掠过我的心头

关节在跳跃

这实在太奇妙

脉搏在加剧

心脏扑扑跳

给你花钱啊小宝贝

我的手脚乱摇

我的心就要爆

你吻我，宝贝，在咖啡店

你让我紧张万分，你得停下

我做了个关于你的梦，宝贝

做了个关于你的梦，宝贝

昨天深夜你旋转着，掠过我的心头

你用一块布包着头

身上穿的长裙是消防车的红色

我做了个关于你的梦，宝贝

做了个关于你的梦，宝贝

昨天深夜你旋转着，掠过我的心头

Had a Dream About You, Baby

I got to see you baby, I don't care
It may be someplace, baby, you say where

I had a dream about you, baby
Had a dream about you, baby
Late last night you come a-rollin' across my mind

You got the crazy rhythm when you walk
You make me nervous when you start to talk

I had a dream about you, baby
Had a dream about you, baby
Late last night you come a-rollin' across my mind

Standin' on the highway, you flag me down
Said, take me Daddy, to the nearest town

I had a dream about you, baby
Had a dream about you, baby
Late last night you come a-rollin' across my mind

The joint is jumpin'
It's really somethin'
The beat is pumpin'
My heart is thumpin'
Spent my money on you honey
My limbs are shakin'
My heart is breakin'

You kiss me, baby, in the coffee shop
You make me nervous, you gotta stop

I had a dream about you, baby
Had a dream about you, baby
Late last night you come a-rollin' across my mind

You got a rag wrapped around your head
Wearing a long dress fire engine red

I had a dream about you, baby
Had a dream about you, baby
Late last night you come a-rollin' across my mind

一夜又一夜

一夜又一夜你漫游在我心灵的街
一夜又一夜不知道你认为你将发现什么
无处可去，无路可走
你周围的一切似乎都在燃烧，燃烧，燃烧
从来就看不到什么悲悯一夜又一夜

一夜又一夜
一夜又一夜

一夜又一夜新的引爆世界的计划
一夜又一夜又一个糟老头吻着某位小姑娘
你寻找着拯救，什么都没找着
只找到又一颗破碎的心，又一支枪管
只找到又一管炸药一夜又一夜

一夜又一夜
一夜又一夜

一夜又一夜你像死人倒在床上
一夜又一夜又一瓶酒找到了宿醉

一夜又一夜我考虑着要让你解脱
但是我不能那样，那样又有何用？
所以我只能将你抱紧一夜又一夜

一夜又一夜
一夜又一夜

Night After Night

Night after night you wander the streets of my mind
Night after night don't know what you think you will find
No place to go, nowhere to turn
Everything around you seems to burn, burn, burn
And there's never any mercy in sight night after night

Night after night
Night after night

Night after night some new plan to blow up the world
Night after night another old man kissing some young girl
You look for salvation, you find none
Just another broken heart, another barrel of a gun
Just another stick of dynamite night after night

Night after night
Night after night

Night after night you drop dead in your bed
Night after night another bottle finds a head
Night after night I think about cutting you loose
But I just can't do it, what would be the use?
So I just keep a-holding you tight night after night

Night after night
Night after night

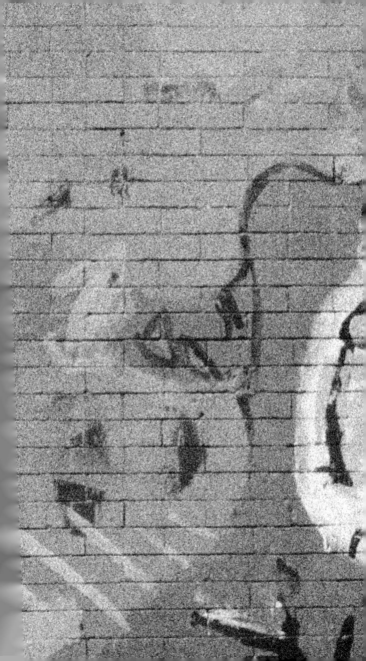

You were always thinking about her
But she slipped away and you lost her trail
And now that you can't do without her
She's back in town like a nightingale
And there ain't gonna be any next time
By now you better understand
That there aint gonna be any next time
So hold her and kiss her and love her while you can

— — — — — — — — — — — — — — — —

哦，仁慈
Oh Mercy

厄土　译

　　《哦，仁慈》是鲍勃·迪伦的第二十六张专辑，发行于 1989 年 9 月，共收录了十二首歌曲。

　　这张专辑在面世不久后便受到了广泛的赞誉，被认为是迪伦在推出了一系列反响不佳的作品后的一次"回归"与"胜利"，其中的一些歌曲更是成了为人所公认的经典之作。在此专辑中，迪伦不但充分地展示了自己的语言天赋，而且在题材的广度和思考的深度上，均取得了明显的突破。无论是《政治世界》《尊严》里对时代颇具讽刺意味的关注与反思，《穿黑大衣的男人》里良知与背叛相互交织的爱情，还是《我有什么好？》里对自我的道德审视与追问，又或是《把钟都敲响吧》里对信仰深刻微妙的思考与暗示，都体现了他丰富而复杂的个人情感。此专辑的整体风格严肃深沉，忧郁失落，颇耐人寻味。

厄土

政治世界

我们活在政治世界里
爱无立锥之地
我们活在人人犯罪的时代里
而罪行无从辨析

我们活在政治世界里
冰柱低垂
婚礼钟声响起，天使高歌
云影遮掩了大地

我们活在政治世界里
智慧被扔进了监狱
它腐烂在囚牢里，被误指成地狱
没给任何人留下可循之迹

我们活在政治世界里
仁慈被迫隐退
生活在镜中，死亡消失
拾阶步入最近的银行里

我们活在政治世界里

勇气已成了陈年旧物

屋里闹鬼，孩子亦属多余

明天可能就是你的末日

我们活在政治世界里

我们能看见也能感受到

但没人会让牌，这是场老千赌局

我们无疑都明白这就是事实

我们活在政治世界里

在寂寞恐惧笼罩的城市里

你渐渐在中途转了向

但你永远都不清楚为何身处此地

我们活在政治世界里

在显微镜底

你可以去任何地方吊死自己

你总能得到绰绰有余的绳子

我们活在政治世界里

翻来覆去

一旦清醒过来，你被训练成

要找看似最简单的路径离开

我们活在政治世界里
这里和平全然不受欢迎
它要么被拒之门外，四处徘徊
要么被逼到墙角里

我们活在政治世界里
所有事物都是她或他的
爬进框架内高喊着上帝之名
但你永远不确定这是怎么回事

Political World

We live in a political world
Love don't have any place
We're living in times where men commit crimes
And crime don't have a face

We live in a political world
Icicles hanging down
Wedding bells ring and angels sing
Clouds cover up the ground

We live in a political world
Wisdom is thrown into jail
It rots in a cell, is misguided as hell
Leaving no one to pick up a trail

We live in a political world
Where mercy walks the plank
Life is in mirrors, death disappears
Up the steps into the nearest bank

We live in a political world
Where courage is a thing of the past
Houses are haunted, children are unwanted
The next day could be your last

We live in a political world
The one we can see and can feel
But there's no one to check, it's all a stacked deck
We all know for sure that it's real

We live in a political world
In the cities of lonesome fear
Little by little you turn in the middle
But you're never sure why you're here

We live in a political world
Under the microscope
You can travel anywhere and hang yourself there
You always got more than enough rope

We live in a political world
Turning and a-thrashing about
As soon as you're awake, you're trained to take
What looks like the easy way out

We live in a political world
Where peace is not welcome at all
It's turned away from the door to wander some more
Or put up against the wall

We live in a political world
Everything is hers or his
Climb into the frame and shout God's name
But you're never sure what it is

泪落之地

远离微风轻拂
远离一切
你动身前往的地方
那就是泪落之地

远离，在暴风雨的夜晚
远离，越过围墙
你在灯火阑珊处
那就是泪落之地

我们缓缓击鼓
我们沉沉奏笛
你知晓我心底的歌
在暮色移转中
在月影里
你可以指给我新的动身之地

我已撕裂了衣服[1]，饮干了杯

1.《圣经》中常用以表达悲痛之情，如《旧约·撒母耳记下》1:2、1:11，有人"衣服撕裂，头蒙灰尘"，来报扫罗等人的死讯，"大卫就撕裂衣服，跟随他的人也是如此"。

抛舍了一切
在日出时思念着你
就在那泪落之地

在盲目的河边
在爱里，怀着善意
如果能够相逢，我们可以一齐举杯
为了突破藩篱
为了让萦绕在火团炽热里的感官
变得敏锐

玫瑰鲜红，紫罗兰幽蓝
时间开始缓慢流逝
也许我应该来见你
就在那泪落之地

Where Teardrops Fall

Far away where the soft winds blow
Far away from it all
There is a place you go
Where teardrops fall

Far away in the stormy night
Far away and over the wall
You are there in the flickering light
Where teardrops fall

We banged the drum slowly
And played the fife lowly
You know the song in my heart
In the turning of twilight
In the shadows of moonlight
You can show me a new place to start

I've torn my clothes and I've drained the cup
Strippin' away at it all
Thinking of you when the sun comes up
Where teardrops fall

By rivers of blindness
In love and with kindness
We could hold up a toast if we meet
To the cuttin' of fences
To sharpen the senses
That linger in the fireball heat

Roses are red, violets are blue
And time is beginning to crawl
I just might have to come see you
Where teardrops fall

一切都已损毁

损毁的线，损毁的绳
损毁的纺丝，损毁的发条
损毁的偶像，损毁的头颅
人们睡在损毁的床上
谎言和玩笑一无所用
一切都已损毁

损毁的瓶子，损毁的餐盘
损毁的开关，损毁的门扇
损毁的餐具，损毁的零件
街上遍布损毁的心灵
损毁的词语从没打算说出口
一切都已损毁

就像你每次驻足回首
总有些什么撞击地面

损毁的刀，损毁的锯
损毁的搭扣，损毁的法律
损毁的身体，损毁的骨头

损毁的电话传来损毁的声音
深吸一口气，就像你已窒息
一切都已损毁

每次你离开，去往某地
事物就碎落在我脸上

损毁的手握着损毁的犁
损毁的条约，损毁的誓言
损毁的管道，损毁的工具
人们屈服于损毁的制度
猎犬咆哮，牛蛙聒噪
一切都已损毁

Everything Is Broken

Broken lines, broken strings
Broken threads, broken springs
Broken idols, broken heads
People sleeping in broken beds
Ain't no use jiving, ain't no use joking
Everything is broken

Broken bottles, broken plates
Broken switches, broken gates
Broken dishes, broken parts
Streets are filled with broken hearts
Broken words never meant to be spoken
Everything is broken

Seem like every time you stop and turn around
Something else just hit the ground

Broken cutters, broken saws
Broken buckles, broken laws
Broken bodies, broken bones
Broken voices on broken phones
Take a deep breath, feel like you're chokin'
Everything is broken

Every time you leave and go off someplace
Things fall to pieces in my face

Broken hands on broken ploughs
Broken treaties, broken vows

Broken pipes, broken tools
People bending broken rules
Hound dog howling, bullfrog croaking
Everything is broken

把钟都敲响吧

把钟都敲响吧
你们自睡梦之城来的外邦人
自众圣所把钟都敲响吧
响彻山谷和溪流
因它们幽深且宽阔
而世界就在它旁边
时光正在回奔
新娘也正是如此

把钟都敲响吧，圣彼得
在四风[1]吹刮的地方
用铁腕把钟都敲响吧
这样人们都会明白
哦，现在是高峰时刻
人们驱着车、负着犁
而太阳即将坠落
在圣牛之上

1.四风，频见于《圣经》，也译作"四方的风"，多指上帝因义怒而降下的惩罚。

把钟都敲响吧，可爱的马大[1]

为穷苦人家的孩子

把钟都敲响吧，这样世界都会明白

上帝只有一位

噢，牧人沉睡了

在杨柳悲泣的地方

山上遍布着

迷途的羔羊

把钟都敲响吧，为了瞎子和聋子

把钟都敲响吧，为我们所有被留下的

把钟都敲响吧，为少数被拣选的

当这场游戏终了，他们要审判众人

把钟都敲响吧，为飞逝的时间

为无罪者死去时

啼哭的孩子

把钟都敲响吧，圣凯瑟琳[2]

从屋顶

---

1. 可爱的马大，伯大尼的马利亚的姐姐，曾接待过耶稣和门徒，为耶稣所喜爱，因为对耶稣的信心，其弟拉撒路死而复活。
2. 圣凯瑟琳，天主教圣人，公元 3 世纪末 4 世纪初的基督教殉道者和圣徒，据传她曾拜访罗马皇帝马克森提乌斯，劝阻其迫害基督徒而被杀害。

也从堡垒上敲钟吧

为盛开的百合

噢，阵线漫长

战斗激烈

而他们打破了

对与错间的距离

Ring Them Bells

Ring them bells, ye heathen
From the city that dreams
Ring them bells from the sanctuaries
'Cross the valleys and streams
For they're deep and they're wide
And the world's on its side
And time is running backwards
And so is the bride

Ring them bells St. Peter
Where the four winds blow
Ring them bells with an iron hand
So the people will know
Oh it's rush hour now
On the wheel and the plow
And the sun is going down
Upon the sacred cow

Ring them bells Sweet Martha
For the poor man's son
Ring them bells so the world will know
That God is one
Oh the shepherd is asleep
Where the willows weep
And the mountains are filled
With lost sheep

Ring them bells for the blind and the deaf
Ring them bells for all of us who are left

Ring them bells for the chosen few
Who will judge the many when the game is through
Ring them bells, for the time that flies
For the child that cries
When innocence dies

Ring them bells St. Catherine
From the top of the room
Ring them from the fortress
For the lilies that bloom
Oh the lines are long
And the fighting is strong
And they're breaking down the distance
Between right and wrong

穿黑大衣的男人

蟋蟀鸣叫，河水高涨
一条柔软的棉裙悬晾在绳上
洞开的窗户，非洲的树
被飓风吹刮得摇曳倒伏
没说一句再见，甚至没留一张便笺
她走了
和那个穿黑大衣的男人

有人曾看见他闲逛
在镇郊的旧舞厅旁
当她拦下他问要不要跳支舞时
他端详她的双眼，他长着一张面具脸
有人用他援引过的《圣经》的话说
那个穿黑大衣的男人
身上满是尘土

那位牧师曾宣讲，他布过一次道
他说："人的天良尽都卑污堕落[1]

1.《新约·提多书》1:15："在污秽不信的人，什么都不洁净，连心地和天良也都污秽了。"

如果需要你去满足它
你就千万不能仰赖于它的引导。"
这话令人难以接受，让人如鲠在喉
她已把真心托付给了
那个穿黑大衣的男人

有人说生活没有错误
有时你确实可以那么想
我赶到了河边，但已错过了那班船
她已经走了
和那个穿黑大衣的男人

从六月开始，水面上总是笼着烟雾
高邈的新月下，树干被连根拔起
感受这脉冲、震颤和轰隆的力
有人在外面拍打一匹死马
她从没说过什么，也没写下什么
她已经走了
和那个穿黑大衣的男人

Man in the Long Black Coat

Crickets are chirpin', the water is high
There's a soft cotton dress on the line hangin' dry
Window wide open, African trees
Bent over backwards from a hurricane breeze
Not a word of goodbye, not even a note
She gone with the man
In the long black coat

Somebody seen him hanging around
At the old dance hall on the outskirts of town
He looked into her eyes when she stopped him to ask
If he wanted to dance, he had a face like a mask
Somebody said from the Bible he'd quote
There was dust on the man
In the long black coat

The preacher was a-talkin', there's a sermon he gave
He said, "Every man's conscience is vile and depraved
You cannot depend on it to be your guide
When it's you who must keep it satisfied."
It ain't easy to swallow, it sticks in the throat
She gave her heart to the man
In the long black coat

There are no mistakes in life some people say
And it's true sometimes you can see it that way
I went down to the river but I just missed the boat
She went with the man
In the long black coat

There's smoke on the water, it's been there since June
Tree trunks uprooted, 'neath the high crescent moon
Feel the pulse and vibration and the rumbling force
Somebody is out there beating on a dead horse
She never said nothing, there was nothing she wrote
She went with the man
In the long black coat

大多数时候

大多数时候
我被周遭瞩目
大多数时候
我都脚踏实地
我能循途守辙，也能读懂路标 [1]
如果道路伸展，我也能保持正确
能应付偶然遇到的事物
我甚至都没留意过她已离去
大多数时候

大多数时候
事情很好理解
大多数时候
我也不会改变，即使我可以
我能让事事如意，能坚持到底
能处理最极端的状况
能挺过去，能忍耐
我甚至都没想起过她

---

1. 读懂路标，双关，亦指察言观色。

大多数时候

大多数时候
我头脑清醒
大多数时候
我足够强大，不怨天尤人
我不会幻想直到这令我恶心
我不惧怕困惑无论它多么严重
我会笑脸迎人
甚至不记得她吻在我双唇的感觉
大多数时候

大多数时候
她甚至不在我的脑海里
就算相遇，我也认不出她
她已那么遥不可及
大多数时候
我甚至无法确定
她是否曾和我在一起
或我是否曾和她在一起

大多数时候
我过得差强人意

大多数时候

我清楚生活去向哪里

我不会自欺，也不会逃避

躲避埋藏于内心的感情

我不会妥协，也不会伪装

我甚至不在意能否和她再次相遇

大多数时候

Most of the Time

Most of the time
I'm clear focused all around
Most of the time
I can keep both feet on the ground
I can follow the path, I can read the signs
Stay right with it when the road unwinds
I can handle whatever I stumble upon
I don't even notice she's gone
Most of the time

Most of the time
It's well understood
Most of the time
I wouldn't change it if I could
I can make it all match up, I can hold my own
I can deal with the situation right down to the bone
I can survive, I can endure
And I don't even think about her
Most of the time

Most of the time
My head is on straight
Most of the time
I'm strong enough not to hate
I don't build up illusion 'til it makes me sick
I ain't afraid of confusion no matter how thick
I can smile in the face of mankind
Don't even remember what her lips felt like on mine
Most of the time

Most of the time
She ain't even in my mind
I wouldn't know her if I saw her
She's that far behind
Most of the time
I can't even be sure
If she was ever with me
Or if I was with her

Most of the time
I'm halfway content
Most of the time
I know exactly where it went
I don't cheat on myself, I don't run and hide
Hide from the feelings that are buried inside
I don't compromise and I don't pretend
I don't even care if I ever see her again
Most of the time

我有什么好？

我有什么好，如果我和其他人一样
如果看到你的衣着我就别过了脸
如果我封闭自己不去听你的哭泣
我有什么好？

我有什么好，如果我知而不行
如果我知而不言，如果我对你视而不见
如果雷鸣滚滚我也充耳不闻
我有什么好？

我有什么好，当你轻声哭泣
我脑海里听到的是你睡梦里的呓语
我就凝固在那一刻像未曾努力的其他人
我有什么好？

我有什么好，无论于人于己
如果我坐拥每个机会但仍未能洞悉
如果我双手被缚是否我就不能好奇
是谁、为何捆缚了我？而我又曾去过何地？

我有什么好，如果我净说蠢话

如果我嘲笑面带愁容的人

如果我在你默默死去时背转身去

我有什么好？

What Good Am I?

What good am I if I'm like all the rest
If I just turn away, when I see how you're dressed
If I shut myself off so I can't hear you cry
What good am I?

What good am I if I know and don't do
If I see and don't say, if I look right through you
If I turn a deaf ear to the thunderin' sky
What good am I?

What good am I while you softly weep
And I hear in my head what you say in your sleep
And I freeze in the moment like the rest who don't try
What good am I?

What good am I then to others and me
If I've had every chance and yet still fail to see
If my hands are tied must I not wonder within
Who tied them and why and where must I have been?

What good am I if I say foolish things
And I laugh in the face of what sorrow brings
And I just turn my back while you silently die
What good am I?

自负之疾

今夜许多人正遭受痛苦
因这自负之疾
今晚许多人正苦苦挣扎
因这自负之疾
一直沿着高速路下来
沿线直下
刺激你的感官
穿透你的肉身和思想
丝毫也不甜蜜
这自负之疾

今夜许多颗心即将破碎
因这自负之疾
今晚许多颗心战栗不休
因这自负之疾
走进你的房间
吞食你的灵魂
凌驾你的感官
你全然无法控制
全无审慎可言

对于这自负之疾

今夜许多人奄奄一息
因这自负之疾
今夜许多人哭喊不止
因这自负之疾
凭空出现
而你一蹶不振
因为外面的世界
压力剧增
会把你压成一片肉饼
这自负之疾

自负是种恶疾
医生也无方可医
他们对此做了许多研究
但这是什么，没人心里有底

今夜许多人陷入困境
因这自负之疾
今晚许多人目有重影
因这自负之疾
给了你自大的妄想

和一只恶眼 [1]

让你认为

自己卓越到不会死亡

而后他们会从头到脚埋葬你

因这自负之疾

1.《旧约·箴言》28:22:"人有恶眼想要急速发财,想要急速发财的,不免受罚。"

Disease of Conceit

There's a whole lot of people suffering tonight
From the disease of conceit
Whole lot of people struggling tonight
From the disease of conceit
Comes right down the highway
Straight down the line
Rips into your senses
Through your body and your mind
Nothing about it that's sweet
The disease of conceit

There's a whole lot of hearts breaking tonight
From the disease of conceit
Whole lot of hearts shaking tonight
From the disease of conceit
Steps into your room
Eats your soul
Over your senses
You have no control
Ain't nothing too discreet
About the disease of conceit

There's a whole lot of people dying tonight
From the disease of conceit
Whole lot of people crying tonight
From the disease of conceit
Comes right out of nowhere
And you're down for the count
From the outside world

The pressure will mount
Turn you into a piece of meat
The disease of conceit

Conceit is a disease
That the doctors got no cure
They've done a lot of research on it
But what it is, they're still not sure

There's a whole lot of people in trouble tonight
From the disease of conceit
Whole lot of people seeing double tonight
From the disease of conceit
Give ya delusions of grandeur
And a evil eye
Give you the idea that
You're too good to die
Then they bury you from your head to your feet
From the disease of conceit

你想要什么？

你想要什么？
再说一遍我才会明白
发生了什么
你的演出是怎么回事
你想要什么
能否再说一次？
我会马上回来
届时你会振作起来

你想要什么？
你可以对我说，我回来了
我们从头开始
让它回到正轨
我注意到了你
说吧，尽管说吧
当你吻我面颊时
你想要什么？

你吻我的时候
有人在看吗

某个阴影里的人
某个我可能忽略了的人?
是否有你想要的东西
某种我无法理解的东西
你想要什么
我手里有吗?

无论你想要什么
它已消失在我脑海里
你能否再提醒我一回
要是你善良如许
唱片是否坏了
刚刚是否跳针了
是否有人正在等待
是否有什么说漏了嘴?

你想要什么
我已无法继续得分
你和之前在这儿的
是同一个人吗?
那是很重要的事吗?
也许不是
你想要什么?

请再次告诉我，我已忘记

无论你要什么
它会是什么
是否有人告诉过你
你能从我这里得到它
它是否理所当然
它是否说来容易
你为何想要它
你究竟是谁？

是否背景在变化
是否我搞错了
是否一切都在倒退
他们在演奏我们的歌吗？
开始的时候你在何处
你想要无条件拥有它吗
你想要什么
你在和我说吗？

What Was It You Wanted?

What was it you wanted?
Tell me again so I'll know
What's happening in there
What's going on in your show
What was it you wanted
Could you say it again?
I'll be back in a minute
You can get it together by then

What was it you wanted
You can tell me, I'm back
We can start it all over
Get it back on the track
You got my attention
Go ahead, speak
What was it you wanted
When you were kissing my cheek?

Was there somebody looking
When you give me that kiss
Someone there in the shadows
Someone that I might have missed?
Is there something you needed
Something I don't understand
What was it you wanted
Do I have it here in my hand?

Whatever you wanted
Slipped out of my mind

Would you remind me again
If you'd be so kind
Has the record been breaking
Did the needle just skip
Is there somebody waiting
Was there a slip of the lip?

What was it you wanted
I ain't keeping score
Are you the same person
That was here before?
Is it something important?
Maybe not
What was it you wanted?
Tell me again I forgot

Whatever you wanted
What could it be
Did somebody tell you
That you could get it from me
Is it something that comes natural
Is it easy to say
Why do you want it
Who are you anyway?

Is the scenery changing
Am I getting it wrong
Is the whole thing going backwards
Are they playing our song?
Where were you when it started
Do you want it for free
What was it you wanted
Are you talking to me?

流星

今夜看到一颗流星
我想到了你
你曾想闯入另一个世界
一片我从未听闻的天地
我一直有些想知道
你是否已经成功
今夜看到一颗流星
我想到了你

今夜看到一颗流星
我想到了自己
是否我依然故我
是否我已变成你想要的我
是否我已迷失了或越过了
只有你看得到的界限？
今夜看到一颗流星
我想到了自己

听啊这引擎，听啊火警钟
当地狱的最后一辆救火车

轰鸣而过

善良的人们都在祈祷

这是最后的诱惑 [1]，最后一笔账 [2]

最后一次你能听到的登山宝训 [3]

最后的广播响起

今夜看到一颗流星

划没天际

明天将是

新的一天

或许已来不及对你说

那些你想从我口中听到的话

今夜看到一颗流星

划没天际

---

1. 最后的诱惑，《新约·马太福音》4，耶稣在旷野受魔鬼的试探。

2. 最后一笔账，多见于《圣经》，意指每个人的罪和义都会被记在他的账上，
在末日审判时每个人都要在上帝面前交账。

3. 登山宝训，指耶稣在山上向众人的宣讲，其中言明了神贫、哀矜、温良、
饥渴慕义、怜悯、心里洁净、缔造和平及为义而受迫害这八种"真福"。

Shooting Star

Seen a shooting star tonight
And I thought of you
You were trying to break into another world
A world I never knew
I always kind of wondered
If you ever made it through
Seen a shooting star tonight
And I thought of you

Seen a shooting star tonight
And I thought of me
If I was still the same
If I ever became what you wanted me to be
Did I miss the mark or overstep the line
That only you could see?
Seen a shooting star tonight
And I thought of me

Listen to the engine, listen to the bell
As the last fire truck from hell
Goes rolling by
All good people are praying
It's the last temptation, the last account
The last time you might hear the sermon on the mount
The last radio is playing

Seen a shooting star tonight
Slip away
Tomorrow will be

Another day
Guess it's too late to say the things to you
That you needed to hear me say
Seen a shooting star tonight
Slip away

一连串的梦

我想起了一连串的梦
那里高处空无一物
一切都处于底部，罹受创伤
进入了一种永息之境
没有想起什么太特别的
就像在梦中，有人醒来尖叫
没有什么太过科学的
只不过想起了一连串的梦

想起了一连串的梦
那里拍子和速度飞驰
四面八方没有一个出口
除了你看不到的那一个
不去建立任何重要的联系
不陷入任何复杂的计划
没有什么能经得住检验
只不过想起了一连串的梦

梦到合上雨伞的地方
在你被扔进的小径里

你手里拿的没有一张好牌

除非它们来自另一个世界

在一个梦中，数字在燃烧

在另一个中，我目睹了一场罪行

在一个梦中，我在飞奔，在另一个中

我仿佛只是在攀登

没有寻求任何特别的援助

也没陷入任何极端的处境

我已然走了很远

只不过想起了一连串的梦

Series of Dreams

I was thinking of a series of dreams
Where nothing comes up to the top
Everything stays down where it's wounded
And comes to a permanent stop
Wasn't thinking of anything specific
Like in a dream, when someone wakes up and screams
Nothing too very scientific
Just thinking of a series of dreams

Thinking of a series of dreams
Where the time and the tempo fly
And there's no exit in any direction
'Cept the one that you can't see with your eyes
Wasn't making any great connection
Wasn't falling for any intricate scheme
Nothing that would pass inspection
Just thinking of a series of dreams

Dreams where the umbrella is folded
Into the path you are hurled
And the cards are no good that you're holding
Unless they're from another world

In one, numbers were burning
In another, I witnessed a crime
In one, I was running, and in another
All I seemed to be doing was climb
Wasn't looking for any special assistance
Not going to any great extremes

I'd already gone the distance
Just thinking of a series of dreams

尊严

体胖者望着一柄钢刀
瘦削者望着他的最后一餐
空腹者望着一片棉田
寻找尊严

智者望着一片草叶
年轻人望着掠过的影子
穷人透过彩色玻璃
寻找尊严

有人被谋杀在新年前夕
有人说尊严最先弃他而去
我走进城中，走进镇里
走进夜半阳光之地

在高地寻觅，在低洼寻觅
在所有我知道的地方寻觅
询问所到之处的警察
你可见到过尊严？

从恍惚中回过神的盲人
把双手伸进了运气的口袋里
希望觅得一件
有关尊严的证据

我去过玛丽·卢的婚礼
她说："我不想任何人看到我和你说话"
说她可能会丧命，如果她告诉我她知道的
关于尊严的事

我曾走入秃鹫的进食之地
我还能去往更深处，但那没什么必要
听天使的话语和人类的话语
于我而言没有什么差异

寒风凛冽犹如刀刃
失火的房子，未偿的债
想去窗边站会儿，想去问问女佣
你可见到过尊严？

饮酒的人倾听他听到的声音
在满是被遮盖的镜子的拥挤房间里
在被遗忘的迷失岁月里

寻找尊严

在蓝调之乡遇到过菲利普亲王
说若他的名字未被使用他会给我来信
他需要现金预付，说他被滥用了
以尊严之名

细沙上奔跑而过的足印
迈向文身之地的脚步
我遇到过黑暗之子和光明之子 [1]
在绝望的边陲小镇

没有地方隐匿，也没有着衣
我在滔滔江面上，在颠簸的小船里
试着阅读某人写的
关于尊严的笔记

病人寻求医生的良方
在他的双手掌纹里
在每一部文学杰作里

1.《新约·帖撒罗尼迦前书》5:5："你们都是光明之子，都是白昼之子；我们
不是属黑夜的，也不是属幽暗的。"

寻找尊严

英国人困在黑心的风里
他正背梳着头发，前途渺茫
他忍着痛苦，在内心中
寻找尊严

有人曾给我看一张照片，我只是笑笑
尊严从未被拍到过
我曾欠过债，曾赚过钱
也曾到过枯骨梦境的山谷 [1]

如此多的路，如此多生死关头
如此多的死胡同，我就在湖边
有时我好奇，该付出什么代价
去寻找尊严

1.《旧约·以西结书》37，以西结看到异象，上帝令枯骨复苏。

Dignity

Fat man lookin' in a blade of steel
Thin man lookin' at his last meal
Hollow man lookin' in a cottonfield
For dignity

Wise man lookin' in a blade of grass
Young man lookin' in the shadows that pass
Poor man lookin' through painted glass
For dignity

Somebody got murdered on New Year's Eve
Somebody said dignity was the first to leave
I went into the city, went into the town
Went into the land of the midnight sun

Searchin' high, searchin' low
Searchin' everywhere I know
Askin' the cops wherever I go
Have you seen dignity?

Blind man breakin' out of a trance
Puts both his hands in the pockets of chance
Hopin' to find one circumstance
Of dignity

I went to the wedding of Mary Lou
She said, "I don't want nobody see me talkin' to you"
Said she could get killed if she told me what she knew
About dignity

I went down where the vultures feed
I would've gone deeper, but there wasn't any need
Heard the tongues of angels and the tongues of men
Wasn't any difference to me

Chilly wind sharp as a razor blade
House on fire, debts unpaid
Gonna stand at the window, gonna ask the maid
Have you seen dignity?

Drinkin' man listens to the voice he hears
In a crowded room full of covered-up mirrors
Lookin' into the lost forgotten years
For dignity

Met Prince Phillip at the home of the blues
Said he'd give me information if his name wasn't used
He wanted money up front, said he was abused
By dignity

Footprints runnin' 'cross the silver sand
Steps goin' down into tattoo land
I met the sons of darkness and the sons of light
In the bordertowns of despair

Got no place to fade, got no coat
I'm on the rollin' river in a jerkin' boat
Tryin' to read a note somebody wrote
About dignity

Sick man lookin' for the doctor's cure
Lookin' at his hands for the lines that were
And into every masterpiece of literature

For dignity

Englishman stranded in the blackheart wind
Combin' his hair back, his future looks thin
Bites the bullet and he looks within
For dignity

Someone showed me a picture and I just laughed
Dignity never been photographed
I went into the red, went into the black
Into the valley of dry bone dreams

So many roads, so much at stake
So many dead ends, I'm at the edge of the lake
Sometimes I wonder what it's gonna take
To find dignity

handy dandy *who was the*
the last thing yu look

1/ handy dandy contrversy always surrounds him *by*
wherefer he goes too bad for him ~~something back that always hounds him~~
hounding ~~pushing~~ him

2. handy dandy he ~~was~~ *is* in a room all ~~just~~ pacing the floor that supports h
in better times anyghing he desired would have just kept walking on
of power ~~pushing~~ toward ~~towrds~~ him *his want here* his respectability dont bot
covering *power*

3. handy dandy ~~a tower of streaght & stability~~ do actually
~~he does it with~~ he dont need to lis cause he's so full of humility
acceseessable *and*

2handy da, compulsive & healty, playsible obsesive automatic
bloin g his horn for the girl ~~hakes~~ & bringing them up tothe attic
for the girl ~~hakes~~ *rubbing them up*
5. handy.... will well yeal mayble ~~has he even sunglasses~~ *Dose he know that he's so plush*
ignorant & blind will al
he ~~knows~~ how much do you weigh *she*
want sul

she ~~some how out of a~~ bone says "tiny lff ben" He says, unbyubbly
6. he's in a rom full ov people and somudeny theres nobody cheering
~~ixxxixxxxhxxxixxhim~~whe says c'mon baby lets both take the wheel to t
car it dont matter~~xhxxx~~ who is steering

红色天空下
Under the Red Sky

李皖　译（郝佳　校）

　　鲍勃·迪伦的《红色天空下》专辑，发行于 1990 年 9 月 10 日，部分创作起因或可归于他的女儿。专辑题献给"盖比咕咕"（Gabby Goo Goo），后来迪伦解释，"盖比咕咕"是他时年四岁女儿的昵称。这导致了一种猜测，这些童谣形式的、时而孩子气十足的作品是迪伦写给他女儿的游戏歌谣。对这种说法，迪伦既未肯定，也未否定。

　　歌词中有大量对英语童谣的引用和摹写，又有诸多对《圣经》素材的移用、改写和变形。通观前后，则有一种整体性：各首歌词之间存在着若有若无、或强或弱的呼应和关联；整张专辑一以贯之，似是对人类命运的关切与忧虑，有着预言和启示录色彩。

　　这是迪伦的第二十七张录音室专辑，与他以前的作品比起来，迪伦完全收起了他备受瞩目的那些做派，改变了形象。滔滔不绝不见了，文字简净乃至于干枯。汪洋恣肆、瑰丽斑斓、天马行空也不见了，暴风骤雨顿歇，烈马收住了缰绳。童谣式的结构乃至部分用语和修辞占据主导，但总体的印象却极为肃静、沉重。循环的节奏和韵律，极简、呈冷暗色调的意象和形象，神秘的人物和情节，具有神圣色彩的警诫和宗教谕示，都通过这种童谣体很好地呈现并凸显出来。

这张专辑另有一个特点是游戏性。游戏性不仅是这些词作的美学特征，还是诸多篇目的灵感和推动力，使得一种近似童话、神话或者谜语的动机、诗境，在游戏中出现并连绵展开，活泼非常，既有天真未知、兴高采烈的欢乐和耍闹，也有置身在外、不动声色、仿似天地不仁的静观和呈示。相伴于歌词，其音乐方面都不怎么舒展，有时枯瘦寡淡，迪伦此前感染力强烈的咆哮与哀鸣，荡然无存。

李皖

扭扭摆摆

扭扭摆摆扭扭摆摆像吉普赛女王
扭扭摆摆扭扭摆摆上上下下着绿装
扭扭摆摆扭扭摆摆直到月亮变成蓝色
扭扭摆摆直到月亮看见你

扭扭摆摆扭扭摆摆穿你的靴你的鞋
扭扭摆摆扭扭摆摆没什么东西会失去
扭扭摆摆扭扭摆摆像一群蜂
扭扭摆摆用你的手和你的膝

扭摆到前，扭摆到后
扭摆直到你扭摆出了这里
扭摆直到它开，扭摆直到它关
扭摆直到它咬，扭摆直到它断

扭扭摆摆扭扭摆摆像一碗汤
扭扭摆摆扭扭摆摆像一个滚环
扭扭摆摆扭扭摆摆像一吨铅
扭扭摆摆——你能使死者复活

扭摆直到你高，扭摆直到你更高

扭摆直到你喷出火

扭摆直到它低语，扭摆直到它哼哼

扭摆直到它回答，扭摆直到它到来

扭扭摆摆扭扭摆摆像缎和绸

扭扭摆摆扭扭摆摆像一桶奶

扭扭摆摆扭摆、摇晃、摇出响声

扭扭摆摆像一条又肥又大的蛇

Wiggle Wiggle

Wiggle, wiggle, wiggle like a gypsy queen
Wiggle, wiggle, wiggle all dressed in green
Wiggle, wiggle, wiggle 'til the moon is blue
Wiggle 'til the moon sees you

Wiggle, wiggle, wiggle in your boots and shoes
Wiggle, wiggle, wiggle, you got nothing to lose
Wiggle, wiggle, wiggle like a swarm of bees
Wiggle on your hands and knees

Wiggle to the front, wiggle to the rear
Wiggle 'til you wiggle right out of here
Wiggle 'til it opens, wiggle 'til it shuts
Wiggle 'til it bites, wiggle 'til it cuts

Wiggle, wiggle, wiggle like a bowl of soup
Wiggle, wiggle, wiggle like a rolling hoop
Wiggle, wiggle, wiggle like a ton of lead
Wiggle—you can raise the dead

Wiggle 'til you're high, wiggle 'til you're higher
Wiggle 'til you vomit fire
Wiggle 'til it whispers, wiggle 'til it hums
Wiggle 'til it answers, wiggle 'til it comes

Wiggle, wiggle, wiggle like satin and silk
Wiggle, wiggle, wiggle like a pail of milk
Wiggle, wiggle, wiggle, rattle and shake
Wiggle like a big fat snake

红色天空 [1] 下

有一个小男孩，有一个小女孩

他们住在一条小巷在红色的天空下

有一个小男孩，有一个小女孩

他们住在一条小巷在红色的天空下

有一个老人住在月亮上

夏日的一天他打此地经过

有一个老人住在月亮上

有一天他打此地经过

有一天小女孩，所有事对你来说将变成新的

有一天小女孩，你将得到像你鞋子一样大的钻石

让风低低吹，让风高高吹

一天小男孩和小女孩双双在一个馅饼中烤着

让风低低吹，让风高高吹

一天小男孩和小女孩双双在一个馅饼中烤着

---

1. 红色天空，见《新约·马太福音》16:1—4。

这是通往王国的钥匙，这是那小镇
这是那匹瞎马它领着你乱转

让鸟儿唱，让鸟儿飞
一天月亮上的人回家了河流变得干涸
让鸟儿唱，让鸟儿飞
月亮上的人回家了河流变得干涸

Under the Red Sky

There was a little boy and there was a little girl
And they lived in an alley under the red sky
There was a little boy and there was a little girl
And they lived in an alley under the red sky

There was an old man and he lived in the moon
One summer's day he came passing by
There was an old man and he lived in the moon
And one day he came passing by

Someday little girl, everything for you is gonna be new
Someday little girl, you'll have a diamond as big as your
    shoe

Let the wind blow low, let the wind blow high
One day the little boy and the little girl were both baked in
    a pie
Let the wind blow low, let the wind blow high
One day the little boy and the little girl were both baked in
    a pie

This is the key to the kingdom and this is the town
This is the blind horse that leads you around

Let the bird sing, let the bird fly
One day the man in the moon went home and the river
    went dry
Let the bird sing, let the bird fly
The man in the moon went home and the river went dry

难以置信

难以置信，这很奇怪却是真的

难以想象，这会发生在你身上

你走向北，你走向南

好像鱼嘴中的诱饵

你肯定生活在哪颗灾星的阴影中

难以置信它可以笼罩得这么远

难以否认他们让你思考的事儿

难以形容，它能驱使你狂饮

他们曾说这里是奶与蜜的土地

现在则说这是金钱的土地

谁曾想他们会说中

难以置信你能这么快这么富裕

每一颗头颅这么庄严

每一颗月亮这么神圣

每一个欲望这么满足，只要你和我在一起

所有的银，所有的金

所有你能拥有的情人

悬挂在一棵树上

不会在未讲的故事中重现

难以置信像一只铅气球[1]
就连学那曲调都非常不可能
杀掉那畜牲喂养那蠢猪
刮掉那墙皮熏死那藤蔓
喂肥骏马把战鼓备上马鞍
难以置信，那一天终将来临

从前有个人他瞎了眼
那片土地上的每个淑女都对他说假话
他站在银色天空下，他的心开始流血
每个大脑都被开化
每根神经都被解析
每件事情都被批评，在你需要帮助的时候

难以置信，无拘无束
如此相互转换，如此赏心悦目
转过你的背，洗干净你的手
总会有人能明白
你说什么都无所谓
难以置信会这样下去

---

1. 像一只铅气球，指毫无用处。

Unbelievable

It's unbelievable, it's strange but true
It's inconceivable it could happen to you
You go north and you go south
Just like bait in the fish's mouth
Ya must be livin' in the shadow of some kind of evil star
It's unbelievable it would get this far

It's undeniable what they'd have you to think
It's indescribable, it can drive you to drink
They said it was the land of milk and honey
Now they say it's the land of money
Who ever thought they could ever make that stick
It's unbelievable you can get this rich this quick

Every head is so dignified
Every moon is so sanctified
Every urge is so satisfied as long as you're with me
All the silver, all the gold
All the sweethearts you can hold
That don't come back with stories untold
Are hanging on a tree

It's unbelievable like a lead balloon
It's so impossible to even learn the tune
Kill that beast and feed that swine
Scale that wall and smoke that vine
Feed that horse and saddle up the drum
It's unbelievable, the day would finally come

Once there was a man who had no eyes
Every lady in the land told him lies
He stood beneath the silver sky and his heart began to bleed
Every brain is civilized
Every nerve is analyzed
Everything is criticized when you are in need

It's unbelievable, it's fancy-free
So interchangeable, so delightful to see
Turn your back, wash your hands
There's always someone who understands
It don't matter no more what you got to say
It's unbelievable it would go down this way

生逢其时

孤独的夜

从闪耀着微蓝光芒的星团

你在黑白中向我袭来

当我们是用梦做成的

你吹过不安的街

你倾听我的心跳

在破纪录的高温中

我们生逢其时

不要再多一夜，不要再多一吻

这一次不了宝贝，再不要这样

需要太多的技巧，需要太多的意志

这实在明显不过

你来了，你看到，就像是法律

你早早结婚，就像你的妈妈

你试了又试，让我滑倒

让我摆脱不了这种感觉

在上升的曲线上

每根神经受到自然规律的考验
你得不到你不应得的
我们生逢其时

你逼我一次，又逼我一次
你悬置那火焰，你将付出代价
噢宝贝，那火
仍在冒烟
你是雪，你是雨
你是条纹的，你是单色的
噢宝贝，没有人说过讲过
比这更真的话

在神秘的山中
在雾蒙蒙的命运之网里
你可以得到残留的我
我们生逢其时

Born in Time

In the lonely night
In the blinking stardust of a pale blue light
You're comin' thru to me in black and white
When we were made of dreams

You're blowing down the shaky street
You're hearing my heart beat
In the record-breaking heat
Where we were born in time

Not one more night, not one more kiss
Not this time baby, no more of this
Takes too much skill, takes too much will
It's revealing
You came, you saw, just like the law
You married young, just like your ma
You tried and tried, you made me slide
You left me reelin' with this feelin'

On the rising curve
Where the ways of nature will test every nerve
You won't get anything you don't deserve
Where we were born in time

You pressed me once, you pressed me twice
You hang the flame, you'll pay the price
Oh babe, that fire
Is still smokin'
You were snow, you were rain

You were striped, you were plain
Oh babe, truer words
Have not been spoken or broken

In the hills of mystery
In the foggy web of destiny
You can have what's left of me
Where we were born in time

关于电视话题的歌

在伦敦城有一次我出外散步
经过一个叫海德公园的地方那儿有人高谈阔论
关于各种不同的神，他们有他们的观点
每一个路人，都是他们谈话的对象

讲台上有人正在向人群演讲
关于电视神及其引起的各种痛苦
"对人的眼睛来说，"他说，"它的光太亮
如果你从没看过它，那似是遗憾，实乃幸福"

我走近前去，踮起脚尖
站我前面的两人正准备动手互殴
台上那男子正在说什么孩子很小
在摇篮曲唱起时就已沦为它的牺牲品

"每时每刻都播着今日新闻
所有最近的八卦，所有最新的歌
心是你的神殿，要让它保持美丽自由
别让你不了解的东西，把它的蛋下在这里头"

"为和平祈祷！"他说。你能够感到人群在应和
我的思想开始漫游。他的调门提得老高
"它将毁掉你的家庭，你快乐的家将失去
一旦你打开它，就没人能保护你"

"它将引你进入奇怪的追逐
带你进入禁果之地
它会搅乱你的头，拖着你的脑子乱走
有时你必须像埃尔维斯那样，把那该死的东西射穿[1]"

"一切都设计好了，"他说，"让人失去头脑
当你想把它找回，却已什么都找不到"
"每次你看着它，你的情况就变得更糟
如果你感到它伸出手抓你，赶紧去叫护士"

人群开始骚动，有人冲过去抓住那男人
大家前推后搡，每个人都在跑
电视摄制组在那儿录像，他们跃过我
当天晚上，我就在电视里看到了这报道

---

1. 有报道说，有一次"猫王"埃尔维斯·普雷斯利在看电视，因电视中播放
的内容引起了他的不快，遂用手枪将电视机击碎。

T.V. Talkin' Song

One time in London I'd gone out for a walk
Past a place called Hyde Park where people talk
'Bout all kinds of different gods, they have their point of
    view
To anyone passing by, that's who they're talking to

There was someone on a platform talking to the folks
About the T.V. god and all the pain that it invokes
"It's too bright a light," he said, "for anybody's eyes
If you've never seen one it's a blessing in disguise"

I moved in closer, got up on my toes
Two men in front of me were coming to blows
The man was saying something 'bout children when they're
    young
Being sacrificed to it while lullabies are being sung

"The news of the day is on all the time
All the latest gossip, all the latest rhyme
Your mind is your temple, keep it beautiful and free
Don't let an egg get laid in it by something you can't see"

"Pray for peace!" he said. You could feel it in the crowd
My thoughts began to wander. His voice was ringing loud
"It will destroy your family, your happy home is gone
No one can protect you from it once you turn it on"

"It will lead you into some strange pursuits
Lead you to the land of forbidden fruits

It will scramble up your head and drag your brain about
Sometimes you gotta do like Elvis did and shoot the damn
    thing out"

"It's all been designed," he said, "to make you lose your
    mind
And when you go back to find it, there's nothing there to
    find
Every time you look at it, your situation's worse
If you feel it grabbing out for you, send for the nurse"

The crowd began to riot and they grabbed hold of the man
There was pushing, there was shoving and everybody ran
The T.V. crew was there to film it, they jumped right over
    me
Later on that evening, I watched it on T.V.

10000 个男人

一万个男人在山上
一万个男人在山上
他们中一些人走下来，一些人将被杀害

一万个男人身穿牛津蓝
一万个男人身穿牛津蓝
在早晨击鼓，在傍晚向你扑来

一万个男人在行进
一万个男人在行进
他们中没人做，你妈妈[1] 不同意的事情

一万个男人挖金掘银
一万个男人挖金掘银
所有人脸刮得干净，所有人不再受冷落

嘿！哪个会是你的爱人？
嘿！哪个会是你的爱人？

---

1. 妈妈，口语中又有"情人""妻子"之意。

让我吃掉他的头，[1] 这样你好真的看清！

一万个女人都一身白衣
一万个女人都一身白衣
站在我的窗前，祝我晚安

一万个男人又瘦又弱
一万个男人又瘦又弱
每一个人娶了七个老婆，每一个人刚刚出狱

一万个女人都打扫着我的房
一万个女人都打扫着我的房
打翻了我的酪乳，用扫帚清理掉

噢宝贝，谢谢你的茶！
宝贝，谢谢你的茶！
你是多么甜，对我多么好

---

1. 英文童谣《一只长尾猪》（*A Long-tailed Pig*）："……抓住他的尾巴，/ 再吃掉他的头，/ 你才能够放心 / 这猪公已死透。"这里的猪乃指猪形状的小吃。

10,000 Men

Ten thousand men on a hill
Ten thousand men on a hill
Some of 'm goin' down, some of 'm gonna get killed

Ten thousand men dressed in oxford blue
Ten thousand men dressed in oxford blue
Drummin' in the morning, in the evening they'll be coming
    for you

Ten thousand men on the move
Ten thousand men on the move
None of them doing nothin' that your mama wouldn't
    disapprove

Ten thousand men digging for silver and gold
Ten thousand men digging for silver and gold
All clean shaven, all coming in from the cold

Hey! Who could your lover be?
Hey! Who could your lover be?
Let me eat off his head so you can really see!

Ten thousand women all dressed in white
Ten thousand women all dressed in white
Standin' at my window wishing me goodnight

Ten thousand men looking so lean and frail
Ten thousand men looking so lean and frail
Each one of 'm got seven wives, each one of 'm just out of jail

Ten thousand women all sweepin' my room
Ten thousand women all sweepin' my room
Spilling my buttermilk, sweeping it up with a broom

Ooh, baby, thank you for my tea !
Baby, thank you for my tea !
It's so sweet of you to be so nice to me

2×2

一个跟着一个，他们追随太阳

一个跟着一个，直到空无一人

两个跟着两个，飞向他们的爱人

两个跟着两个，进入雾蒙蒙的露水

三个跟着三个，他们在海上跳舞

四个跟着四个，他们在岸边跳舞

五个跟着五个，他们试图活下去

六个跟着六个，他们玩着把戏

有多少路他们试过而失败了？

有多少他们的兄弟姐妹苟活在监狱？

有多少毒气他们吸进去？

有多少黑猫穿过了他们的小路？

七个跟着七个，他们前往天堂

八个跟着八个，他们到了门口

九个跟着九个，他们喝酒

十个跟着十个，他们再喝

有多少明天被他们虚掷？

有多少明天与昨日相比？

还有多少明天无任何回报？

还有多少明天可供他们挥霍？

两个跟着两个，他们走进方舟

两个跟着两个，他们步入黑暗

三个跟着三个，他们在转动钥匙

四个跟着四个，他们又再转动

一个跟着一个，他们追随太阳

两个跟着两个，去下一个集合地

2×2

One by one, they followed the sun
One by one, until there were none
Two by two, to their lovers they flew
Two by two, into the foggy dew
Three by three, they danced on the sea
Four by four, they danced on the shore
Five by five, they tried to survive
Six by six, they were playing with tricks

How many paths did they try and fail?
How many of their brothers and sisters lingered in jail?
How much poison did they inhale?
How many black cats crossed their trail?

Seven by seven, they headed for heaven
Eight by eight, they got to the gate
Nine by nine, they drank the wine
Ten by ten, they drank it again

How many tomorrows have they given away?
How many compared to yesterday?
How many more without any reward?
How many more can they afford?

Two by two, they stepped into the ark
Two by two, they step in the dark
Three by three, they're turning the key
Four by four, they turn it some more

One by one, they follow the sun
Two by two, to another rendezvous

上帝知道

上帝知道你不漂亮
上帝知道这是真的
上帝知道没有任何人
要取代你的位置

上帝知道这是场困斗
上帝知道这是桩罪行
上帝知道不会再是水了
下一回会是火

上帝不把它叫背叛
上帝不把它叫犯错
它本该延续一个季节
可它坚挺了这么久

上帝知道它脆弱
上帝知道一切
上帝知道它能马上断成两截
就像一根线遇上了一把剪子

上帝知道它恐怖吓人

上帝看到一切已呈现

有一百万个理由让你哭

你已变得如此大胆，如此冷酷

上帝知道当你看见它

上帝知道你一定会流泪

上帝知道你心里那些秘密

当你睡着的时候，他会把它们告诉你

上帝知道有一条河

上帝知道如何让它流动

上帝知道你带不走任何东西

在你离去的时候

上帝知道有一个目的

上帝知道有一次机会

上帝知道你能战胜最黑暗的时刻

在任何情况下

上帝知道有个天堂

上帝知道它在看不见的地方

上帝知道我们能从这一直走到那

即使趁着烛光，走一百万英里

God Knows

God knows you ain't pretty
God knows it's true
God knows there ain't anybody
Ever gonna take the place of you

God knows it's a struggle
God knows it's a crime
God knows there's gonna be no more water
But fire next time

God don't call it treason
God don't call it wrong
It was supposed to last a season
But it's been so strong for so long

God knows it's fragile
God knows everything
God knows it could snap apart right now
Just like putting scissors to a string

God knows it's terrifying
God sees it all unfold
There's a million reasons for you to be crying
You been so bold and so cold

God knows that when you see it
God knows you've got to weep
God knows the secrets of your heart
He'll tell them to you when you're asleep

God knows there's a river
God knows how to make it flow
God knows you ain't gonna be taking
Nothing with you when you go

God knows there's a purpose
God knows there's a chance
God knows you can rise above the darkest hour
Of any circumstance

God knows there's a heaven
God knows it's out of sight
God knows we can get all the way from here to there
Even if we've got to walk a million miles by candlelight

猜手手公子 [1]

猜手手公子，周围全是议论
他环游了世界，又回来
月光中有什么还在追逐他
猜手手公子，就像糖块与糖果

猜手手公子，就算他每一根骨头都折了，他也不会承认
他有一个全女子管弦乐队，当他说
"开始演奏。"她们就演奏
猜手手公子，猜手手公子

你说："你是用什么东西做的？"
他说："你能重复一遍问题吗？"
你会说："什么是你惧怕的？"
他会说："没有！无论生还是死。"

猜手手公子，他手里抓着拐杖，口袋里装满钱

---

1. 歌名源自一种儿童游戏。一人双手成拳，让别人猜哪只手里攥有小物件。
猜前双拳快速上下互绕，念带有"猜手手公子"一语之类的童谣，然后双拳上
下相叠让人猜。

他说："亲爱的，告诉我实情，我有多少时间？"

她说："你有世界上所有的时间，亲爱的"

猜手手公子，猜手手公子

他有水晶般清澈的喷泉

他有丝绸般柔软的皮肤

他有山顶的城堡

没有门，没有窗，没有贼人能闯入

猜手手公子，跟一个叫南希的女孩，懒洋洋坐在花园里

他说："你要支枪吗？我给你。"她说："天哪，你疯了吗"

猜手手公子，就像糖块与糖果

猜手手公子，再给他倒杯白兰地

猜手手公子，他得到一篮子花和一袋子忧伤

他喝光杯子里的酒，从座位上站起来，说

"好了，孩子们，咱们明天见"

猜手手公子，猜手手公子，就像糖块与糖果

猜手手公子，就像糖块与糖果

Handy Dandy

Handy Dandy, controversy surrounds him
He been around the world and back again
Something in the moonlight still hounds him
Handy Dandy, just like sugar and candy

Handy Dandy, if every bone in his body was broken he
    would never admit it
He got an all-girl orchestra and when he says
"Strike up the band," they hit it
Handy Dandy, Handy Dandy

You say, "What are ya made of?"
He says, "Can you repeat what you said?"
You'll say, "What are you afraid of?"
He'll say, "Nothin'! Neither 'live nor dead."

Handy Dandy, he got a stick in his hand and a pocket full
    of money
He says, "Darling, tell me the truth, how much time I got?"
She says, "You got all the time in the world, honey"
Handy Dandy, Handy Dandy

He's got that clear crystal fountain
He's got that soft silky skin
He's got that fortress on the mountain
With no doors, no windows, no thieves can break in

Handy Dandy, sitting with a girl named Nancy in a garden
    feelin' kind of lazy

He says, "Ya want a gun? I'll give ya one." She says, "Boy,
   you talking crazy"
Handy Dandy, just like sugar and candy
Handy Dandy, pour him another brandy

Handy Dandy, he got a basket of flowers and a bag full of
   sorrow
He finishes his drink, he gets up from the table, he says
"Okay, boys, I'll see you tomorrow"
Handy Dandy, Handy Dandy, just like sugar and candy
Handy Dandy, just like sugar and candy

猫在井下

猫在井下，狼在上面看着
猫在井下，狼在上面看着
他毛蓬蓬的大尾巴满地拖

猫在井下，温柔的女士睡了
猫在井下，温柔的女士睡了
她什么也听不见，寂静包围着她

猫在井下，悲伤露出它的脸
世界正被屠戮，这是怎样一个该死的耻辱

猫在井下，马儿颠颠儿地颠
猫在井下，马儿颠颠儿地颠
后巷里的莎莉在玩"美国蹦"[1]

猫在井下，爸爸在读新闻
他的头发在脱落，他的女儿们都需要鞋

-----

1. 美国蹦，大人抓着小孩的手蹦跳的游戏。

猫在井下，棚里满是公牛

猫在井下，棚里满是公牛

夜这样长，桌子啊这样满

猫在井下，仆人在门边

酒准备好了，狗将投入战斗

猫在井下，树叶开始落了

猫在井下，树叶开始落了

晚安，我的爱，愿上帝怜悯我们

Cat's in the Well

The cat's in the well, the wolf is looking down
The cat's in the well, the wolf is looking down
He got his big bushy tail dragging all over the ground

The cat's in the well, the gentle lady is asleep
Cat's in the well, the gentle lady is asleep
She ain't hearing a thing, the silence is a-stickin' her deep

The cat's in the well and grief is showing its face
The world's being slaughtered and it's such a bloody
    disgrace

The cat's in the well, the horse is going bumpety bump
The cat's in the well, and the horse is going bumpety bump
Back alley Sally is doing the American jump

The cat's in the well, and Papa is reading the news
His hair's falling out and all of his daughters need shoes

The cat's in the well and the barn is full of bull
The cat's in the well and the barn is full of bull
The night is so long and the table is oh, so full

The cat's in the well and the servant is at the door
The drinks are ready and the dogs are going to war

The cat's in the well, the leaves are starting to fall
The cat's in the well, leaves are starting to fall
Goodnight, my love, may the Lord have mercy on us all

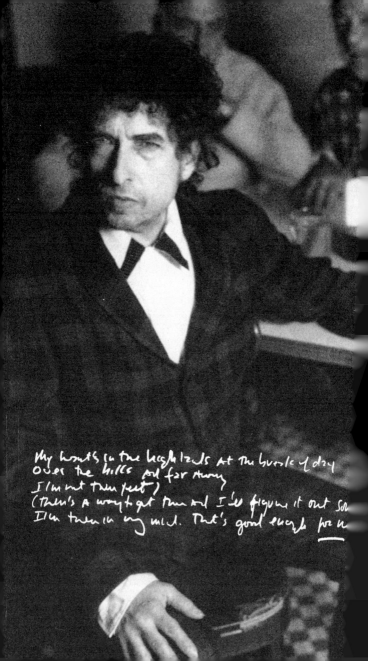

My heart's in the highlands at the break of day
Over the hills and far away
(I'm not there yet)
(there's a way to get there and I'll figure it out some
I'm there in my mind. That's good enough for n

被遗忘的时光
Time Out of Mind

陈震 译

1997 年，鲍勃·迪伦推出了他的第三十张录音室专辑《被遗忘的时光》。20 世纪 80 年代，无论是音乐事业还是健康状况，迪伦都陷入了低谷。进入 90 年代后，更是连续七年没有发表原创专辑。到 1997 年时，迪伦已经五十六岁了，年岁渐长的他又开始面临衰老之苦。所以谁都没有料到，这张《被遗忘的时光》会成为迪伦的强势复出之作，让他东山再起，踏上不可思议的重返巅峰之路。除了一举拿下包括 1998 年度最佳专辑在内的三项格莱美奖，《被遗忘的时光》还入选《滚石》杂志评出的史上最佳五百张专辑。这张专辑重新奠定了他在乐坛的地位，也让新一代乐迷认识了他的价值。

彼时，即将步入老年的诗人又一次身处人生的十字路口。像许多五十六岁的男人一样，他会不自觉地回首过往，心头泛起悔恨和忧伤，而面对衰老和未来，又会陷入烦恼和焦躁。

《被遗忘的时光》根植于蓝调的土壤中，是迪伦的一次心灵之旅，睿智、内省而平和，个中亦夹杂着心碎和苦楚。他退回到了充满悔恨和忧伤的私人世界中，我们能在里面听到错失爱情的懊悔、对情爱的不灭渴望和"夜幕将垂"式的感慨。尖锐的鼻音呐喊经常被缓慢而深沉的吟唱取代。

《被遗忘的时光》为迪伦的后期作品定下了一个基调，其后期作品的高水准一直保持至今。

陈震

相思成疾

我走过死气沉沉的街
边走，边想你
我的双脚好疲惫，我的大脑好迷醉
云朵在流泪

我听到有人在说谎？
我听到远处有人哭泣？
你让我的心狂喜，再把它撕碎
你翻我的口袋，当我在安睡

我厌恶爱情……但我深陷里面
这种爱情……让我那么生厌

我看见草地上的情侣
我看见窗户上的轮廓
我看着他们，直到离开我的视线
留给我握紧，一道阴影

我厌恶爱情……我听到钟摆滴答滴
我厌恶爱情……我相思成疾

有时寂静如响雷

有时我觉得自己被击溃

你能真诚待我？我在想着你

我想搞清楚

我厌恶爱情……我后悔遇到你

我厌恶爱情……我竭力忘掉你

只是六神无主

我愿付出全部，只为与你相依

Love Sick

I'm walking through streets that are dead
Walking, walking with you in my head
My feet are so tired, my brain is so wired
And the clouds are weeping

Did I hear someone tell a lie?
Did I hear someone's distant cry?
You thrilled me to my heart, then you ripped it all apart
You went through my pockets when I was sleeping

I'm sick of love… but I'm in the thick of it
This kind of love… I'm so sick of it

I see lovers in the meadow
I see silhouettes in the window
I watch them 'til they're gone and they leave me hanging on
To a shadow

I'm sick of love… I hear the clock tick
I'm sick of love… I'm love sick

Sometimes the silence can be like the thunder
Sometimes I feel like I'm being plowed under
Could you ever be true? I think of you
And I wonder

I'm sick of love… I wish I'd never met you
I'm sick of love… I'm trying to forget you

Just don't know what to do
I'd give anything to just be with you

泥土路蓝调

我将沿着那条泥土路走，直到有人搭我一程
我将沿着那条泥土路走，直到有人搭我一程
如果找不到我的宝贝儿，我会逃走躲起来

我在屋里踱来踱去，希望她会回来
我在屋里踱来踱去，希望她会回来
噢，我躺在一间乡下棚屋，祈祷着灵魂得救

我将沿着那条泥土路走，直到我的眼睛鲜血直流
我将沿着那条泥土路走，直到我的眼睛鲜血直流
直到没有什么可看，直到镣铐被砸断，我得到自由

我盯着我的影子，望着天空的色彩
我盯着我的影子，望着天空的色彩
穿过雨水和冰雹，寻找爱情的阳光

我将沿着那条泥土路走，直到太阳的近旁
我将沿着路一直走，直到太阳的近旁
我得打造一个障碍，把我和所有人隔开

Dirt Road Blues

Gon' walk down that dirt road, 'til someone lets me ride
Gon' walk down that dirt road, 'til someone lets me ride
If I can't find my baby, I'm gonna run away and hide

I been pacing around the room hoping maybe she'd
    come back
Pacing 'round the room hoping maybe she'd come back
Well, I been praying for salvation laying 'round in a
    one-room country shack

Gon' walk down that dirt road until my eyes begin to bleed
Gon' walk down that dirt road until my eyes begin to bleed
'Til there's nothing left to see, 'til the chains have been
    shattered and I've been freed

I been lookin' at my shadow, I been watching the colors
    up above
Lookin' at my shadow, watching the colors up above
Rolling through the rain and hail, looking for the sunny side
    of love

Gon' walk on down that dirt road 'til I'm right beside
    the sun
Gon' walk on down until I'm right beside the sun
I'm gonna have to put up a barrier to keep myself away
    from everyone

伫立门口

我走过夏夜

点唱机低声吟唱

昨天光阴似箭

今天度日如年

我无处可去

无物可焚

如果遇见你，不知会吻你还是杀你

不过你也许毫不在意

你留下我伫立门口哭泣

我已回不到往昔

这里的光线糟糕透顶

让我头晕恶心

笑声徒增悲伤

繁星已变樱桃红

我扫着欢乐的吉他

抽着廉价的雪茄

旧情的魂灵尚未离开

看起来不像急着要走

你留下我伫立门口哭泣

在午夜的月下

他们也许会来抓我也许不会
但不是今晚也不在这里
有些事我能说但不说
我知道主的仁慈就在隔壁
我乘着午夜列车
血管里流着冰水
如果让你回到我身边，那我真是疯了
这有悖于一切常规
你留下我伫立门口哭泣
遭罪得像个傻子

当最后几道余晖下沉
老兄，你将不再滚动
我听见教堂的钟声在院里响起
我想知道它们为谁而鸣
我知道我不可能赢
但我的心不会认输
昨夜我与陌生人共舞
但她只让我想到你才是唯一
你留下我伫立门口哭泣
在太阳的黑暗之地

饿了就吃，渴了就喝
诚实坦率地过我的生活
即使皮肉从我脸上脱落
我知道有人会关心我
这对我总是意味着太多
即使是最轻柔的触摸
什么解释都无济于事
什么言语都无需启齿
你留下我伫立门口哭泣
忧伤包裹着我的头

Standing in the Doorway

I'm walking through the summer nights
Jukebox playing low
Yesterday everything was going too fast
Today, it's moving too slow
I got no place left to turn
I got nothing left to burn
Don't know if I saw you, if I would kiss you or kill you
It probably wouldn't matter to you anyhow
You left me standing in the doorway crying
I got nothing to go back to now

The light in this place is so bad
Making me sick in the head
All the laughter is just making me sad
The stars have turned cherry red
I'm strumming on my gay guitar
Smoking a cheap cigar
The ghost of our old love has not gone away
Don't look like it will anytime soon
You left me standing in the doorway crying
Under the midnight moon

Maybe they'll get me and maybe they won't
But not tonight and it won't be here
There are things I could say but I don't
I know the mercy of God must be near
I've been riding the midnight train
Got ice water in my veins
I would be crazy if I took you back

It would go up against every rule
You left me standing in the doorway crying
Suffering like a fool

When the last rays of daylight go down
Buddy, you'll roll no more
I can hear the church bells ringing in the yard
I wonder who they're ringing for
I know I can't win
But my heart just won't give in
Last night I danced with a stranger
But she just reminded me you were the one
You left me standing in the doorway crying
In the dark land of the sun

I'll eat when I'm hungry, drink when I'm dry
And live my life on the square
And even if the flesh falls off of my face
I know someone will be there to care
It always means so much
Even the softest touch
I see nothing to be gained by any explanation
There are no words that need to be said
You left me standing in the doorway crying
Blues wrapped around my head

百万英里

你带走了我的一部分，我真的想念它
我不停地追问自己，这样下去还能持续多久
你对自己说了谎，没关系妈妈，我也对自己说了一个
我试着靠近你，但离你还有一百万英里

你带走了银子，带走了金子
把我丢在寒冷中站立
人们问起你，我没有告诉他们我所知道的东西
噢，我试着靠近你，但离你还有一百万英里

我飘进飘出无梦的睡乡
把所有记忆扔进深深的沟渠
做了那么多从没打算做的事
噢，我试着靠近你，但离你还有一百万英里

我渴望你的爱，调暗你的灯吧
我需要每一点每一滴，给我要去的地方
有时我想知道会走到哪步田地
噢，我试着靠近你，但离你还有一百万英里

噢，我不敢闭眼也不敢眨眼

也许我下辈子能集中注意力

想跟别人聊天，却不知道跟谁聊

噢，我试着靠近你，但离你还有一百万英里

你启程前撂下最后一句话

"我去寻个能把我迷倒的保洁员"

我说："那好吧，做你该做的"

噢，我试着靠近你，但离你还有一百万英里

摇摆我吧，漂亮宝贝儿，摇摆到一切变得真实

摇摆我一小会儿，摇摆到失去所有感觉

然后我也会摇摆你

我试着靠近你，但离你还有一百万英里

噢，夜里有说话声想被听见

我坐在这里，听着每一个玷污心灵的词

我知道很多人会留我住一两天

是的，我试着靠近你，但离你还有一百万英里

Million Miles

You took a part of me that I really miss
I keep asking myself how long it can go on like this
You told yourself a lie, that's all right mama I told myself
    one too
I'm tryin' to get closer but I'm still a million miles from you

You took the silver, you took the gold
You left me standing out in the cold
People asked about you, I didn't tell them everything
    I knew
Well, I'm tryin' to get closer but I'm still a million miles
    from you

I'm drifting in and out of dreamless sleep
Throwing all my memories in a ditch so deep
Did so many things I never did intend to do
Well, I'm tryin' to get closer but I'm still a million miles
    from you

I need your love so bad, turn your lamp down low
I need every bit of it for the places that I go
Sometimes I wonder just what it's all coming to
Well, I'm tryin' to get closer but I'm still a million miles
    from you

Well, I don't dare close my eyes and I don't dare wink
Maybe in the next life I'll be able to hear myself think
Feel like talking to somebody but I just don't know who

Well, I'm tryin' to get closer but I'm still a million miles
from you

The last thing you said before you hit the street
"Gonna find me a janitor to sweep me off my feet"
I said, "That's all right, you do what you gotta do"
Well, I'm tryin' to get closer, I'm still a million miles from
you

Rock me, pretty baby, rock me 'til everything gets real
Rock me for a little while, rock me 'til there's nothing left to
feel
And I'll rock you too
I'm tryin' to get closer but I'm still a million miles from you

Well, there's voices in the night trying to be heard
I'm sitting here listening to every mind-polluting word
I know plenty of people who would put me up for a day or
two
Yes, I'm tryin' to get closer but I'm still a million miles from
you

试图进入天堂

天气越来越热

天空隆隆作响

我在高涨的泥水中蹚行

眼中热力升腾

你的记忆一天天变得模糊

不再像以前那样缠扰着我

我穿行在穷乡僻壤

试图进入天堂，趁大门还没关上

当我在密苏里时

他们不让我做自己

我得匆忙离开

我只看到了他们让我看到的

你伤了一颗爱你的心

现在你可以封上你的书，不再写下来

我在走那寂寞山谷

试图进入天堂，趁大门还没关上

月台上的人

等待列车

我能听到他们的心在跳

如钟摆来回摆动

你心里渴望的所有

我都尽力给你

我沿着这条路走，心里很难受

试图进入天堂，趁大门还没关上

我顺流而下

到新奥尔良

他们告诉我一切都会没事的

但我不知道"没事的"是什么意思

我与玛丽·珍小姐同乘一车

玛丽·珍小姐在巴尔的摩有栋房

我周游了世界，小伙子们

现在我试图进入天堂，趁大门还没关上

将在客厅里睡一觉

重温我的梦想

我会闭上眼睛

琢磨一切是否如看到的那样空洞

当你以为已经失去一切

却发现总还有一点可以失去

我去过糖镇，我摇落树上的糖

现在我试图进入天堂，趁大门还没关上

Tryin' to Get to Heaven

The air is getting hotter
There's a rumbling in the skies
I've been wading through the high muddy water
With the heat rising in my eyes
Every day your memory grows dimmer
It doesn't haunt me like it did before
I've been walking through the middle of nowhere
Trying to get to heaven before they close the door

When I was in Missouri
They would not let me be
I had to leave there in a hurry
I only saw what they let me see
You broke a heart that loved you
Now you can seal up the book and not write anymore
I've been walking that lonesome valley
Trying to get to heaven before they close the door

People on the platforms
Waiting for the trains
I can hear their hearts a-beatin'
Like pendulums swinging on chains
I tried to give you everything
That your heart was longing for
I'm just going down the road feeling bad
Trying to get to heaven before they close the door

I'm going down the river
Down to New Orleans

They tell me everything is gonna be all right
But I don't know what "all right" even means
I was riding in a buggy with Miss Mary-Jane
Miss Mary-Jane got a house in Baltimore
I been all around the world, boys
Now I'm trying to get to heaven before they close the door

Gonna sleep down in the parlor
And relive my dreams
I'll close my eyes and I wonder
If everything is as hollow as it seems
When you think that you've lost everything
You find out you can always lose a little more
I been to Sugar Town, I shook the sugar down
Now I'm trying to get to heaven before they close the door

直到爱上了你

噢，我的神经在爆炸，躯体在紧张

我感觉整个世界把我钉在了篱笆上

我受到了严重的打击，看清了太多

现在没有什么可以治愈我，除了你的抚摸

我不知所措

我没问题，直到爱上了你

噢，我的房子在燃烧，燃烧到天际

我以为会下雨，但云朵一飘而过

我感觉已经走投无路

但我知道上帝是我的庇护，他不会让我误入歧途

我仍不知所措

我没问题，直到爱上了你

街上的男孩开始嬉戏

女孩像鸟一样飞离

我走了你会记得我的名字

我会一路去赢得名利

我不知所措

我没问题，直到爱上了你

杂物堆积，占着地方
我的眼睛像要从脸上掉落
汗滴坠下，我盯着地板
想着那个女孩一去不返
我不知所措
我没问题，直到爱上了你

好吧，我厌倦了交谈，厌倦了解释
我再取悦你都是枉然
明晚太阳落山前
如果我还在人世间，我将去往老南方
我只是不知所措
我没问题，直到爱上了你

'Til I Fell in Love with You

Well, my nerves are exploding and my body's tense
I feel like the whole world got me pinned up against the
  fence
I've been hit too hard, I've seen too much
Nothing can heal me now, but your touch
I don't know what I'm gonna do
I was all right 'til I fell in love with you

Well, my house is on fire, burning to the sky
I thought it would rain but the clouds passed by
Now I feel like I'm coming to the end of my way
But I know God is my shield and he won't lead me astray
Still I don't know what I'm gonna do
I was all right 'til I fell in love with you

Boys in the street beginning to play
Girls like birds flying away
When I'm gone you will remember my name
I'm gonna win my way to wealth and fame
I don't know what I'm gonna do
I was all right 'til I fell in love with you

Junk is piling up, taking up space
My eyes feel like they're falling off my face
Sweat falling down, I'm staring at the floor
I'm thinking about that girl who won't be back no more
I don't know what I'm gonna do
I was all right 'til I fell in love with you

Well, I'm tired of talking, I'm tired of trying to explain
My attempts to please you were all in vain
Tomorrow night before the sun goes down
If I'm still among the living, I'll be Dixie bound
I just don't know what I'm gonna do
I was all right 'til I fell in love with you

天还未暗

驻足一日，夜幕下垂
时光溜走，热不能寐
感觉灵魂，已变钢铁
太阳无法，抚平伤疤
无论哪里，都很拥挤
天还未暗，但已不远

我的仁心，付之东流
美丽背后，苦痛常存
她的来信，如此友善
心中所想，付于纸上
干吗介怀，我不明白
天还未暗，但已不远

去过伦敦，浪过巴黎
沿河而下，到达海洋
谎言世界，底部一游
眼中之物，非我所求
有些重担，无法承受
天还未暗，但已不远

生死于斯，虽非我愿
看似奔走，实则未动
每根神经，麻木茫然
逃避什么，才来这里
喃喃祈祷，都听不到
天还未暗，但已不远

Not Dark Yet

Shadows are falling and I've been here all day
It's too hot to sleep, time is running away
Feel like my soul has turned into steel
I've still got the scars that the sun didn't heal
There's not even room enough to be anywhere
It's not dark yet, but it's getting there

Well, my sense of humanity has gone down the drain
Behind every beautiful thing there's been some kind of pain
She wrote me a letter and she wrote it so kind
She put down in writing what was in her mind
I just don't see why I should even care
It's not dark yet, but it's getting there

Well, I've been to London and I've been to gay Paree
I've followed the river and I got to the sea
I've been down on the bottom of a world full of lies
I ain't looking for nothing in anyone's eyes
Sometimes my burden seems more than I can bear
It's not dark yet, but it's getting there

I was born here and I'll die here against my will
I know it looks like I'm moving, but I'm standing still
Every nerve in my body is so vacant and numb
I can't even remember what it was I came here to get away
    from
Don't even hear a murmur of a prayer
It's not dark yet, but it's getting there

被冰冷的镣铐束缚

我听见了说话声，可四下无人
噢，我力气用光，田野已变黄
我周日去教堂，她经过我身旁
我对她的爱，那么久才亡

我在齐腰深的、齐腰深的薄雾中
几乎就像、几乎就像消失无踪
我在城外二十英里处，被冰冷的镣铐束缚

自尊之墙又高又宽
看不到另一端
看到美貌衰败真让人伤心
更让人伤心的是你变了心

一见你我就失控
像宇宙吞噬了我的全部
我在城外二十英里处，被冰冷的镣铐束缚

太多、太多的人可以忆起
我以为有些人是我的朋友，我全看走了眼

道路崎岖，山坡泥泞
我的头顶只有血云

我找到了我的世界，在你里面
但你的爱没被证明是真爱
我在城外二十英里处，被冰冷的镣铐束缚
城外二十英里处，被冰冷的镣铐束缚

哦，芝加哥的风把我撕成碎片
现实总长着许多脑袋
有些东西的命比你想象的硬
有种东西你永远杀不死

我在想你，我只在想你
但你看不到里面，我也看不到外面
我在城外二十英里处，被冰冷的镣铐束缚

嗯，肥肉在火焰里，水在水箱里
威士忌在杯子里，钱在银行里
我努力去爱你保护你，因为我在乎你
我会永远记住，我们分享的欢喜

我单膝跪地看着你

你不知道你怎样对待我的

我在城外二十英里处，被冰冷的镣铐束缚

城外二十英里处，被冰冷的镣铐束缚

Cold Irons Bound

I'm beginning to hear voices and there's no one around
Well, I'm all used up and the fields have turned brown
I went to church on Sunday and she passed by
My love for her is taking such a long time to die

I'm waist deep, waist deep in the mist
It's almost like, almost like I don't exist
I'm twenty miles out of town in cold irons bound

The walls of pride are high and wide
Can't see over to the other side
It's such a sad thing to see beauty decay
It's sadder still to feel your heart torn away

One look at you and I'm out of control
Like the universe has swallowed me whole
I'm twenty miles out of town in cold irons bound

There's too many people, too many to recall
I thought some of 'm were friends of mine, I was wrong
   about 'm all
Well, the road is rocky and the hillside's mud
Up over my head nothing but clouds of blood

I found my world, found my world in you
But your love just hasn't proved true
I'm twenty miles out of town in cold irons bound
Twenty miles out of town in cold irons bound

Oh, the winds in Chicago have torn me to shreds
Reality has always had too many heads
Some things last longer than you think they will
There are some kind of things you can never kill

It's you and you only I been thinking about
But you can't see in and it's hard lookin' out
I'm twenty miles out of town in cold irons bound

Well the fat's in the fire and the water's in the tank
The whiskey's in the jar and the money's in the bank
I tried to love and protect you because I cared
I'm gonna remember forever the joy that we shared

Looking at you and I'm on my bended knee
You have no idea what you do to me
I'm twenty miles out of town in cold irons bound
Twenty miles out of town in cold irons bound

让你感受到我的爱

当雨水打湿你的脸庞
当全世界都在数落你
我会给你一个温暖的拥抱
让你感受到我的爱

当夜幕降临，繁星初现
无人为你擦干眼泪
我会抱你千秋万载
让你感受到我的爱

我知道你心意未决
但我永远不会错待你
从我们相遇的那一刻起
我就明了我心所属

我饥肠辘辘，伤痕累累
我在大街上爬行
愿为你做任何事情
让你感受到我的爱

翻滚的大海上，悔恨的公路上

暴风雨肆虐

把手交给我跟我走

我来确保你不被雨淋

我会让你快乐满盈，让你梦想成真

愿为你做任何事情

愿为你去世界尽头

让你感受到我的爱

Make You Feel My Love

When the rain is blowing in your face
And the whole world is on your case
I could offer you a warm embrace
To make you feel my love

When the evening shadows and the stars appear
And there is no one there to dry your tears
I could hold you for a million years
To make you feel my love

I know you haven't made your mind up yet
But I would never do you wrong
I've known it from the moment that we met
No doubt in my mind where you belong

I'd go hungry, I'd go black and blue
I'd go crawling down the avenue
There's nothing that I wouldn't do
To make you feel my love

The storms are raging on the rollin' sea
And on the highway of regret
Put your hand in mine and come with me
I'll see that you don't get wet

I could make you happy, make your dreams come true
Nothing that I wouldn't do
Go to the ends of the earth for you
To make you feel my love

等不及

我等不及，等不及你回心转意
时间已晚，我试着保持镇定
哦，子夜已过，到处是人
有的下降，有的上升
空气在燃烧，我在理清头脑
我不知道还能等多久

我是你的男人，试图找回我俩甜蜜的爱
你知道，没了你我的心会停摆
你的美丽伤害了我，我被击打得晕头转向
真想知道为何还那么爱你
我使劲呼吸，站在门口
但我不知道还能等多久

天空昏暗，我在寻找每一缕幸福感
白天夜晚，去哪都行，我只管去
如若看到你走来，我会不知所措
我倒想控制住自己，但我做不到
事物分崩离析时就是这样
我不知道还能等多久

我注定爱你，我在暴风雨中一路前进
我在想你，和所有我们能一起漫步之地

简直太滑稽，时间的尽头才开启
哦，亲爱的，多年过去你仍是我的唯一
当我漫步在我的心灵孤墓
我会回到路上的某处，把生命交给你
这样就能免遭今天的运数
但我不知道还能等多久

Can't Wait

I can't wait, wait for you to change your mind
It's late, I'm trying to walk the line
Well, it's way past midnight and there are people all around
Some on their way up, some on their way down
The air burns and I'm trying to think straight
And I don't know how much longer I can wait

I'm your man, I'm trying to recover the sweet love that we
knew
You understand that my heart can't go on beating without
you
Well, your loveliness has wounded me, I'm reeling from the
blow
I wish I knew what it was keeps me loving you so
I'm breathing hard, standing at the gate
But I don't know how much longer I can wait

Skies are grey, I'm looking for anything that will bring a
happy glow
Night or day, it doesn't matter where I go anymore, I just
go
If I ever saw you coming I don't know what I would do
I'd like to think I could control myself, but it isn't true
That's how it is when things disintegrate
And I don't know how much longer I can wait

I'm doomed to love you, I've been rolling through stormy
weather
I'm thinking of you and all the places we could roam together

It's mighty funny, the end of time has just begun
Oh, honey, after all these years you're still the one
While I'm strolling through the lonely graveyard of my
    mind
I left my life with you somewhere back there along the line
I thought somehow that I would be spared this fate
But I don't know how much longer I can wait

高地

哦，我的心在高地[1]，温柔而合理
金银花在原始林的空气里绽放
风铃草在阿伯丁的水流中闪耀
哦，我的心在高地
我会去那里，当我心情够好

梦里的窗户摇了一晚上
一切正是该有的模样
今晨醒来，我看着同样的旧篇章
同样的你争我夺
同样的笼里生活

我不想要任何人的东西，没多少是我需要的
不知道真金发女郎和冒牌金发女郎有何区别
感觉就像一个囚犯在一个神秘的世界
希望有人前来
为我把时光倒转

---

1. 源自苏格兰诗人罗伯特·彭斯（Robert Burns）诗歌《我的心在高地》
（*My Heart's in the Highlands*）。

哦，无论走到哪里，我的心都在高地
当归家的讯号响起，我就会去那里
风，对着七叶树低语着韵文
哦，我的心在高地
只有一步一个脚印，我才能到达那里

我在听尼尔·杨[1]，我得开大音量
有人老嚷嚷"别开那么响"
我有漂泊之感
从一个圈漂到另一个圈
我想知道这到底是什么意思？

疯癫打砸着我的灵魂
你可以说我万事不顺
如果我有良心，我会怒发冲冠
我该怎么对待良心呢
也许把它带到当铺

破晓时分，我的心在高地
美丽的黑天鹅湖边

—————————

1. 尼尔·杨（Neil Young，1945— ），与鲍勃·迪伦齐名的加拿大摇滚
音乐家。

大朵的白云像双轮马车般垂荡

哦，我的心在高地

剩下唯一要去的地方

我在波士顿城，一家餐馆里

不知道来点什么

哦，也许我知道，但我真的不确定

女招待走了过来

这里只有我和她

一定是假日，周围再没旁人

当我坐下时，她仔细打量我

她有张漂亮的脸蛋，有双修长光滑的白腿

她问："来点什么？"

我说："不知道，有溏心蛋吗？"

她看着我说："我想给你端来的

但是已经没了，你来得不是时候"

然后她说："我知道你是艺术家，给我画一幅画！"

我说："如果我可以，我会给你画，但

我不凭记忆画"

"噢，"她说，"我就在你面前，你没看到？"

我说："好吧，我知道，但我没有图画本！"

她给我一块餐巾，说："你可以在这上面画"

我说："是的，我可以，但

我不知道我的铅笔在哪里！"

她从她耳朵后面抽出一支

说："好了，来吧，画我，我就站在这儿"

我画了几笔给她看

她接过餐巾又扔回来

说："一点不像我！"

我说："哦，体贴的小姐，当然很像"

她说："你在开玩笑吧。"我说："我倒希望是！"

然后她说："你不读女作家，是吧？"

至少我记得她是这么说的

"好吧，"我说，"你怎么知道？这重要吗？"

"嗯，"她说，"你看起来不像！"

我说："你大错特错"

她说："那你读过谁的？"我说："埃丽卡·容[1]！"

---

1. 埃丽卡·容（Erica Jong，1942— ），美国女作家、诗人，其小说《怕飞》
（*Fear of Flying*）被认为在第二波女性主义运动中占有重要地位。

她离开了一分钟

我滑下椅子

走回外面，街上熙熙攘攘，但人们漫无方向

哦，我的心在高地，与马和犬一起

远在边境乡村，远离城镇

与箭的弦声和弓的啪声一起

我的心在高地

看不到其他任何路可走

外面天天一成不变

感觉我离自己越来越远

有些东西想学为时已晚

哦，我在哪儿迷失了

一定是做了几个坏决定

我看见公园里的人们忘记了烦恼和悲伤

他们喝酒跳舞，穿着鲜艳的衣裳

年轻的男人和他们年轻的女人真好看啊

哦，我会和他们中的任何人交换身份

马上，如果我能

我过马路躲一条癞皮狗

跟自己唠叨
我想我需要的也许是一件皮大衣
有人问我
有没有登记投票

阳光开始照在我身上
但它和以往的不一样
派对已结束，越来越没话讲
我有了新的眼睛
一切看上去都很遥远

哦，破晓时分，我的心在高地
在山上在远方
有条路通往那里，我会把它琢磨透
但我的心已在那里
现在这已足够

Highlands

Well my heart's in the Highlands, gentle and fair
Honeysuckle blooming in the wildwood air
Bluebells blazing where the Aberdeen waters flow
Well my heart's in the Highlands
I'm gonna go there when I feel good enough to go

Windows were shakin' all night in my dreams
Everything was exactly the way that it seems
Woke up this morning and I looked at the same old page
Same ol' rat race
Life in the same ol' cage

I don't want nothing from anyone, ain't that much to take
Wouldn't know the difference between a real blonde and
    a fake
Feel like a prisoner in a world of mystery
I wish someone would come
And push back the clock for me

Well my heart's in the Highlands wherever I roam
That's where I'll be when I get called home
The wind, it whispers to the buck-eyed trees in rhyme
Well my heart's in the Highlands
I can only get there one step at a time

I'm listening to Neil Young, I gotta turn up the sound
Someone's always yelling turn it down
Feel like I'm drifting
Drifting from scene to scene

I'm wondering what in the devil could it all possibly mean?

Insanity is smashing up against my soul
You can say I was on anything but a roll
If I had a conscience, well, I just might blow my top
What would I do with it anyway
Maybe take it to the pawn shop

My heart's in the Highlands at the break of dawn
By the beautiful lake of the Black Swan
Big white clouds like chariots that swing down low
Well my heart's in the Highlands
Only place left to go

I'm in Boston town, in some restaurant
I got no idea what I want
Well, maybe I do but I'm just really not sure
Waitress comes over
Nobody in the place but me and her

It must be a holiday, there's nobody around
She studies me closely as I sit down
She got a pretty face and long white shiny legs
She says, "What'll it be?"
I say, "I don't know, you got any soft boiled eggs?"

She looks at me, says, "I'd bring you some
But we're out of 'm, you picked the wrong time to come"
Then she says, "I know you're an artist, draw a picture of
    me !"
I say, "I would if I could, but
I don't do sketches from memory"

"Well," she says, "I'm right here in front of you, or haven't
   you looked?"
I say, "All right, I know, but I don't have my drawing
   book!"
She gives me a napkin, she says, "You can do it on that"
I say, "Yes I could, but
I don't know where my pencil is at!"

She pulls one out from behind her ear
She says, "All right now, go ahead, draw me, I'm standing
   right here"
I make a few lines and I show it for her to see
Well she takes the napkin and throws it back
And says, "That don't look a thing like me!"

I said, "Oh, kind Miss, it most certainly does"
She says, "You must be jokin'." I say, "I wish I was!"
Then she says, "You don't read women authors, do you?"
Least that's what I think I hear her say
"Well," I say, "how would you know and what would it
   matter anyway?"

"Well," she says, "you just don't seem like you do!"
I said, "You're way wrong"
She says, "Which ones have you read then?" I say, "I read
   Erica Jong!"
She goes away for a minute
And I slide up out of my chair
I step outside back to the busy street but nobody's going
   anywhere

Well my heart's in the Highlands with the horses and
   hounds

Way up in the border country, far from the towns
With the twang of the arrow and a snap of the bow
My heart's in the Highlands
Can't see any other way to go

Every day is the same thing out the door
Feel further away than ever before
Some things in life, it gets too late to learn
Well, I'm lost somewhere
I must have made a few bad turns

I see people in the park forgetting their troubles and woes
They're drinking and dancing, wearing bright-colored
    clothes
All the young men with their young women looking
    so good
Well, I'd trade places with any of them
In a minute, if I could

I'm crossing the street to get away from a mangy dog
Talking to myself in a monologue
I think what I need might be a full-length leather coat
Somebody just asked me
If I registered to vote

The sun is beginning to shine on me
But it's not like the sun that used to be
The party's over and there's less and less to say
I got new eyes
Everything looks far away

Well, my heart's in the Highlands at the break of day
Over the hills and far away

There's a way to get there and I'll figure it out somehow
But I'm already there in my mind
And that's good enough for now

桑田沧海

忧虑的男人怀着忧虑的心
身前无人，身后无物
喝着香槟的女人坐在我怀中
皮肤白皙，眼睛含血
我仰望着蓝宝石色的天空
一身光鲜地等待末班列车

我站在绞刑架上，头套在绞索里
随时等待着灾难降临

疯掉的人们，吊诡的时代
我被紧紧锁住，我在范围之外
我曾经在乎，但已桑田沧海

这地方对我没有好处
我待错了地方，我应该在好莱坞
有那么一瞬，我感觉有人在动
去上舞蹈课，学跳吉特巴
没有捷径可走，得扮女人逗乐
只有傻子才认为需要向他人证明什么

桥下有好多水，还有好多其他东西
不用起身，先生，我只是个过客

疯掉的人们，吊诡的时代
我被紧紧锁住，我在范围之外
我曾经在乎，但已桑田沧海

我走了四十英里破路
如果《圣经》是对的，那这世界会爆炸
我尽可能地远离自己
有些东西烫得不能碰
人心只能承受那么多
一手烂牌怎能成赢家

感觉爱上了遇见的第一个女人
把她放在独轮车里沿街推行

疯掉的人们，吊诡的时代
我被紧紧锁住，我在范围之外
我曾经在乎，但已桑田沧海

我容易受伤，我只是不流露
你会伤害到别人而毫无觉察

下一个六十秒会很漫长

将要伏下，将要高飞

世上的所有真相加起来是一个弥天大谎

我爱上了一个对我没有吸引力的女人

金克斯先生和露西小姐跳进湖中

我没那么急着要犯错

疯掉的人们，吊诡的时代

我被紧紧锁住，我在范围之外

我曾经在乎，但已桑田沧海

Things Have Changed

A worried man with a worried mind
No one in front of me and nothing behind
There's a woman on my lap and she's drinking champagne
Got white skin, blood in my eyes
I'm looking up into the sapphire-tinted skies
I'm well dressed, waiting on the last train

Standing on the gallows with my head in a noose
Any minute now I'm expecting all hell to break loose

People are crazy and times are strange
I'm locked in tight, I'm out of range
I used to care, but things have changed

This place ain't doing me any good
I'm in the wrong town, I should be in Hollywood
Just for a second there I thought I saw something move
Gonna take dancing lessons, do the jitterbug rag
Ain't no shortcuts, gonna dress in drag
Only a fool in here would think he's got anything to prove

Lot of water under the bridge, lot of other stuff too
Don't get up gentlemen, I'm only passing through

People are crazy and times are strange
I'm locked in tight, I'm out of range
I used to care, but things have changed

I've been walking forty miles of bad road

If the Bible is right, the world will explode
I've been trying to get as far away from myself as I can
Some things are too hot to touch
The human mind can only stand so much
You can't win with a losing hand

Feel like falling in love with the first woman I meet
Putting her in a wheelbarrow and wheeling her down the
    street

People are crazy and times are strange
I'm locked in tight, I'm out of range
I used to care, but things have changed

I hurt easy, I just don't show it
You can hurt someone and not even know it
The next sixty seconds could be like an eternity
Gonna get low down, gonna fly high
All the truth in the world adds up to one big lie
I'm in love with a woman who don't even appeal to me

Mr. Jinx and Miss Lucy, they jumped in the lake
I'm not that eager to make a mistake

People are crazy and times are strange
I'm locked in tight, I'm out of range
I used to care, but things have changed

红河岸

我们中有些人关掉灯
我们躺在倾泻的月光下
黑暗中，待在这天使飞翔的地方
我们中有些人把自己吓得要死
漂亮的姑娘们排成一行
在我的小屋门外
我一点也不希望她们中有人对我有意思
除了来自红河岸边的姑娘

哦，我坐在她身旁，试图
让她成为我的妻子
她给了我最好的建议，说
回家过太平日子
哦，我去过东部，去过西部
去过黑风呼啸的地方
可不知怎的，我从没走到那一步
和来自红河岸边的姑娘

哦，第一眼见到她我就知晓
我永远都自由不了

瞥她一眼立刻知道

她应该永远和我在一起

哦，那个梦很久前就已枯竭

不知道它现在哪里

真诚过活，真心待我

来自红河岸边的姑娘

哦，我披着痛苦的斗篷

尝着被抛弃的爱情

僵在脸上的微笑

合身得像只手套

但我逃不开记忆里

我永远深爱的唯一

那些躺在她怀里的晚上

来自红河岸边的姑娘

哦，我们活在褪色过往的阴影里

困在时光的火焰中

我努力不去伤害任何人

远离犯罪之路

当一切尘埃落定

我却从未知道实情

多过去一天就又分开一天

和来自红河岸边的姑娘

哦，这儿是异乡，我是异客
可我知道它是我的归宿
我为爱人去游荡去冒险
群山会给我一首歌
一切看着都不眼熟
但我知道我曾在此驻足
那是一千个夜晚之前
和来自红河岸边的姑娘

哦，我回去找过她
回去把事情理顺
我问的每个人都见过我们
却都说不知道我在说谁
哦，太阳很久前就已沉落
似乎不再发光
但愿能共度每一个日出日落
和来自红河岸边的姑娘

我听说很久以前有个家伙
充满了悲伤和冲突
如果他身边有人亡故

他知道如何让他复活

哦，我不知道他使用哪种语言

或者他们还做那种事不

有时我觉得这儿压根没人见过我

除了来自红河岸边的姑娘

Red River Shore

Some of us turn off the lights and we lay
Up in the moonlight shooting by
Some of us scare ourselves to death in the dark
To be where the angels fly
Pretty maids all in a row lined up
Outside my cabin door
I've never wanted any of 'em wanting me
'Cept the girl from the Red River shore

Well I sat by her side and for a while I tried
To make that girl my wife
She gave me her best advice when she said
Go home and lead a quiet life
Well I been to the East and I been to the West
And I been out where the black winds roar
Somehow, though, I never did get that far
With the girl from the Red River shore

Well I knew when I first laid eyes on her
I could never be free
One look at her and I knew right away
She should always be with me
Well the dream dried up a long time ago
Don't know where it is anymore
True to life, true to me
Was the girl from the Red River shore

Well I'm wearing the cloak of misery
And I've tasted jilted love

And the frozen smile upon my face
Fits me like a glove
But I can't escape from the memory
Of the one that I'll always adore
All those nights when I lay in the arms
Of the girl from the Red River shore

Well we're livin' in the shadows of a fading past
Trapped in the fires of time
I tried not to ever hurt anybody
And to stay out of a life of crime
And when it's all been said and done
I never did know the score
One more day is another day away
From the girl from the Red River shore

Well I'm a stranger here in a strange land
But I know this is where I belong
I ramble and gamble for the one I love
And the hills will give me a song
Though nothing looks familiar to me
I know I've stayed here before
Once a thousand nights ago
With the girl from the Red River shore

Well I went back to see about her once
Went back to straighten it out
Everybody that I talked to had seen us there
Said they didn't know who I was talkin' about
Well the sun went down a long time ago
And doesn't seem to shine anymore
I wish I could have spent every hour of my life
With the girl from the Red River shore

Now I heard of a guy who lived a long time ago
A man full of sorrow and strife
That if someone around him died and was dead
He knew how to bring him on back to life
Well I don't know what kind of language he used
Or if they do that kind of thing anymore
Sometimes I think nobody ever saw me here at all
'Cept the girl from the Red River shore